COUP DE GRÂCE

50
FARRAR
STRAUS
GIROUX

BY MARGUERITE YOURCENAR

NOVELS AND SHORT STORIES

Alexis ou le traité du vain combat, 1929;
in English, *Alexis*, 1984
La nouvelle Eurydice, 1931
Denier du rêve, 1934; revised edition, 1959;
in English, *A Coin in Nine Hands*, 1982
Nouvelles orientales, 1938; revised edition, 1963, 1978;
in English, *Oriental Tales*, 1985
Le coup de grâce, 1939; in English, *Coup de Grâce*, 1957
Mémoires d'Hadrien, 1951; in English, *Memoirs of Hadrian*, 1954
L'oeuvre au noir, 1968; in English, *The Abyss*, 1976
Comme l'eau qui coule, 1982;
in English, *Two Lives and a Dream*, 1987

POEMS AND PROSE POEMS

Feux, 1936; in English, *Fires*, 1981
Les charités d'Alcippe, 1956
Blues et gospels, 1984; photographs by Jerry Wilson

DRAMA

Théâtre I, 1971
Théâtre II, 1971

ESSAYS AND AUTOBIOGRAPHY

Pindare, 1932
Les songes et les sorts, 1938
Sous bénéfice d'inventaire, 1962;
in English, *The Dark Brain of Piranesi*, 1984
Discours de réception de Marguerite Yourcenar
à l'Académie Royale belge, 1971
Le labyrinthe du monde I: Souvenirs pieux, 1974;
in English, *Dear Departed*, 1991
Le labyrinthe du monde II: Archives du nord, 1977;
in English, *How Many Years*, 1995
Le labyrinthe du monde III: Quoi? L'éternité, 1988
Mishima ou la vision du vide, 1980;
in English, *Mishima: A Vision of the Void*, 1986
Discours de réception à l'Académie Française
de Mme M. Yourcenar, 1981
Le temps, ce grand sculpteur, 1983;
in English, *That Mighty Sculptor, Time*, 1992

Coup de Grâce

MARGUERITE YOURCENAR

Translated from the French by Grace Frick
in Collaboration with the Author

The Noonday Press
Farrar, Straus and Giroux
New York

First published in French in 1939 under the title *Le coup de grâce*
by Editions Gallimard, Paris

Published in Canada by HarperCollins*CanadaLtd*
Printed in the United States of America
Library of Congress catalog card number: 57-10687
Designed by Marshall Lee
First published in English in 1957 by Farrar, Straus and Cudahy
This edition first published in 1981 by The Noonday Press
Tenth printing, 1997

Preface

This short novel, translated from the French, has its setting in the aftermath of the War of 1914–18, and of the Russian Revolution. It was written in Italy, at Sorrento, in 1938, and was published just three months before the outbreak of the Second World War, thus some twenty years later than the incidents which it relates. The subject matter may now seem remote because so many episodes of other civil wars have been superposed upon those events in the intervening years, but it is close to us, too, because we are still plunged (and more deeply than ever) into the moral disorder depicted therein. The story itself is authentic, and the three characters who are called Erick, Sophie, and Conrad, respectively, remain much as they were described to me by one of the best friends of the principal person concerned.

The whole episode was moving to me, as I hope it will be to the reader. Furthermore, and from a literary point of view alone, it seemed to me to encompass all the structural elements of classical tragedy, and therefore to fit admirably into the framework of traditional French récit, retaining, as this form does, certain characteristics of French classical tragedy, unity of time, of place, and, as Corneille once felicitously defined it, unity of danger. Likewise, the action limited to two or three persons, of whom one, at least, was sufficiently clear-sighted to strive to comprehend, and pass judgment on, himself. Finally, the episode contained within itself the inevitable tragic ending toward which passion always tends, but which ordinarily assumes, in daily life, more secret or more insidious forms. Even the setting, that faraway corner of Baltic territory, isolated by revolution and war, seemed to meet the requirements of tragic drama by freeing Sophie's and Erick's story from what would be for us the usual contingencies, and providing us with that remoteness in space which is almost the equivalent of distance in time. (Such was the reasoning of Racine, carefully set forth in his preface to Bajazet, a tragedy of *events close to his own time but occurring in what was then the closed world of the Ottoman Empire.)*

It was not my intention in writing this book to re-create a particular social group or period, unless to do so incidentally. But the psychological truth which we seek is bound up too much today with what is individual and specific to allow us with good conscience, as did our classical models before us, to remain ignorant of, or to pass over, the external realities which govern a situation. The place which I call Kratovitsy has to be more than the stylized setting for classical tragedy, and the gory episodes of civil war have to be shown as more than a vague red backdrop for a love tale; for what had happened in that place had reduced these characters to a state of permanent despair which alone explains their actions. This young man and young girl unknown to me except for a brief résumé of their story could plausibly exist for us only if set in that exact lighting, and, in so far as possible, in circumstances historically correct. Thus this subject primarily chosen for its basic conflict between individual passions and wills eventually forced me to pore over ordinance maps, to seek out details given by other eyewitnesses, and to scan old illustrated magazines in order to catch the least echo or reflection which might have reached Western Europe at the time that those obscure military operations were taking place on a for-

gotten frontier. More than once since the book appeared, men who had fought in those Baltic wars have graciously volunteered to tell me that *Coup de Grâce* corresponds to their own memories of those years. Naturally, no critical article, however favorable, has ever reassured me more as to the substance of one of my books.

The account is written in the first person as if narrated by the principal character, a method to which I have often resorted because it eliminates the author's point of view from the book, or at least his comments, and allows a human being to be shown looking squarely upon his own life, trying first of all to recall it entire, and more or less honestly to explain it. Let us bear in mind, however, that a long oral recital made by the central figure of a novel to willing, silent listeners is, after all, a literary device: that the hero should tell his story with such precision of detail and such discursive logic is possible, say, in *The Kreutzer Sonata* or in *The Immoralist*, but not in real life: actual confessions are apt to be more fragmentary, or more repetitive, more confused or more vague. Such reservations hold, of course, for the narration which the hero of *Coup de Grâce* proffers to somewhat inattentive comrades during a long wait in a railway station.

Nevertheless, this initial convention once conceded, it depends upon the author of such a *récit* to put into it the whole of a being, with all his qualities and defects as revealed in his own peculiarities of expression, with his judgments sound or false, his prejudices unknown to him, his lies, which may reveal truths, and his avowals, which may lie, his reticences, and even his lapses of memory.

But this literary form, more than any other, has the inconvenience of demanding strict collaboration from the reader, obliging him to rectify, as for objects seen through water, persons and events as presented to him by the character who is speaking. In most cases, this bias of a *récit* in first person favors the speaker; in *Coup de Grâce*, on the contrary, the inevitable deformation which occurs when one talks of oneself works to the detriment of the narrator. A man like Erick von Lhomond habitually questions his own motives; his horror of duping himself inclines him, in case of doubt, to offer the least favorable interpretation of his actions; his fear of exposing his feelings locks him in harshness like a cuirass, though no man truly harsh would ever don such a protection; his very pride makes him constantly play down his self-esteem. In consequence, a naïve reader might make a sadist of Erick, not recognizing in him a man resolved to confront even the most atrocious of his memories; or might see him merely as a brute in military brass, precisely forgetting that no brute would ever be haunted by recollections of having caused suffering.

And such a reader would mistake for a professional anti-Semite this aristocrat whose habitual irony toward Jews is a matter of caste, but who reveals his admiration for the courage of the Jewish moneylender, and who elevates her son, Gregory Loew, to the heroic circle of friends and enemies already lost in death.

This disparity between what the narrator tells of himself, and what he truly is, or has been, is most marked, as might be expected, in the complex relations where both love and hatred are at play. If Erick seems to relegate Conrad de Reval to second place, offering only a rather vague portrait of this friend so ardently loved, it is because, first of all, he is not one to insist upon what he cares for most, and next because there is not much to say to these indifferent auditors about a comrade lost young, before reaching adulthood. Possibly, in a few of Erick's allusions to his friend, an alert listener would have caught that tone of assumed unconcern, or of barely perceptible irritation, that one feels for someone too deeply cherished. If, on the contrary, he gives first place in his narrative to Sophie, depicting her sympathetically even in her errings and her tragic excesses, it is not merely because the young girl's love flatters or reassures him; it is because his code obliges him to treat with respect that adversary that every woman becomes for a man whom she loves but who does not love her.

Other such slantings are less voluntary on Erick's part. This man ordinarily so lucid in his thinking unintentionally rationalizes the fervors and refusals which were those of early youth: perhaps he had been more in love with Sophie than he says; he was surely more jealous of her than his vanity allows him to admit. On the other hand, his repugnance and his revolt in presence of the young girl's compelling ardor are less rare than he supposes them to be, and are almost routine effects of shock from a man's first encounter with love's terrifying force.

Beyond the story of the girl who offers herself and the young man who holds himself aloof, the central subject of Coup de Grâce is the community of temperament and of destiny shared by these three beings subjected to the same privations and the same dangers. Erick and Sophie especially are alike in their intransigence, and in their passion to carry experience through to its end. Sophie's violence stems from the need to surrender herself body and soul to another, much more than from desire to be possessed by some chance lover, or to seduce him. Erick's devotion to Conrad is more than physical or even sentimental; his choice is really aligned with a certain ideal of austerity, born of chivalric dreams of comradeship, and is part of his whole view on life; even his concept of love is one aspect of his discipline.

When Erick and Sophie meet again at the end of the

book, through the few words they find worth exchanging I have tried to show that particular intimacy or affinity which is stronger than either conflicts of political allegiances or physical passions, and even stronger than rancors of wounded vanity or frustrated desire. This fast bond unites them, whatever they may do, and explains the depths of their wounds. At the point where they now stand it matters little which of the two deals death to the other, or which one is the victim. It even matters little whether or not they loved or hated each other.

One reason for choosing to write *Coup de Grâce* (though I know that I inscribe myself against contemporary fashion in saying so) is the intrinsic *nobility* of its characters. Let us be clear, however, about the meaning of this word, which signifies for me total absence of self-interest or calculation. Of course, there is danger of equivocation in speaking of nobility in a book where the three principal characters belong to a privileged caste, of which they are the last representatives. We know only too well that the two concepts of moral nobility and aristocracy of class are not always superposed upon each other, far from it. On the other hand, we fall into current popular prejudice in denying that the notion of nobility of blood (however artificial the ideal) has sometimes helped to develop in certain natures those qualities of independence or pride, loyalty and disinteredness *which are, by definition, noble. In any case, this inherent dignity (which contemporary literature by sheer convention seldom grants to its characters) is so little a matter of social origin that Erick, in spite of his prejudices, concedes it to Gregory Loew, but denies it to the scheming Volkmar, who is nevertheless of Erick's same background and political associations.*

With regret for having to underline, in closing, what ought to be apparent, I should mention that Coup de Grâce *does not aim at exalting or discrediting any one group or class, any country or party. The very fact that I have deliberately given Erick von Lhomond a French name and French ancestors (perhaps in order to credit him with that sharp lucidity which is not a particularly German trait) precludes any interpretation of him as either an idealized portrait or a caricature of one type of German officer or aristocrat. It is for value as a human, not political, document (if it has value), that* Coup de Grâce *has been written and accordingly should be judged.*

COUP DE GRÂCE

It was five in the morning, and pouring rain; Erick von Lhomond sat waiting in the station buffet at Pisa for the train which was to take him back to Germany. He had been wounded at Saragossa, and was just off an Italian hospital ship. Though nearly forty, he seemed young, as if his kind of hard, youthful elegance would never change; the narrow profile bespoke French ancestry, but his mother was Balt and his father Prussian, hence the pale blue eyes, the tall stature, the arrogant smile and the heel-click, the latter now in abeyance, of course, because of his fractured and bandaged foot. It was close to that hour between dark and dawn when men of feeling confide and criminals confess, and when even the least loquacious among us try to fend off sleep by story after story, or by summoning up the past.

Von Lhomond was one of those men who were too young in 1914 to have done more than brush with danger, but who were transformed into soldiers of fortune by Europe's post-war disorders, and by their personal anxieties as well, their incapacity for satisfaction or resignation, either one. Any cause half-lost, half-won attracted them. Neither by birth nor by inclination was Erick disposed to the leftist side: he had taken part in the various movements in Central Europe which culminated in the rise of Hitler, and had turned up in the Chaco and in Manchuria before serving under Franco in Spain; and much earlier he had led a corps of volunteers against the Bolsheviks in Kurland. Now his wounded foot, virtually swaddled, was resting across a chair, and as he talked he absently fingered an old-fashioned gold watch of such size and style that the wearer could only be admired for his courage in displaying the heirloom on his wrist. On his right hand he wore a massive ring, engraved with a family crest. He had a way of striking the table from time to time, not with his fist but with the flat of his palm, repeatedly startling his comrades and setting the glasses a-tingle. That sound, in turn, would awaken the chubby Italian waiter, asleep behind the counter. Over and over again the strangers were solicited, most unseasonably, by an old beggar of a coachman, blind in one eye and dripping from rain, who kept coming to propose a drive to the Leaning Tower. The German had to break off more than once in his story to drive the wretch sharply away, and one of the two auditors would make use of the interval to call for coffee again; a cigarette case would snap shut, and the narrator, suddenly overcome and utterly worn out, would bend over his lighter, momentarily suspending the interminable confession which he was making, in reality, to no one but himself.

"Fast go the dead," as the German ballad has it, but so do the living, too. After fifteen years I can scarcely recall just what did happen in that confused struggle against the Bolsheviks in Livonia and Kurland, in that whole corner of the civil war with its hidden complications and sudden eruptions, like a fire not quite put out, or some skin disease. Each region, for that matter, has its own kind of war, a local product like rye or potatoes.

The fullest ten months of my life were passed in a

command in that godforsaken district where even the names, Russian, Lettish, Germanic, meant nothing to newspaper readers in Europe or anywhere else: a land of lakes, birch forest, beet fields and small, dreary towns or lice-ridden villages where our men sometimes had the luck to butcher a pig; of old estates with their vast houses stripped bare within and pockmarked without by bullets where the owners and their families had been lined up and shot; of Jewish money-lenders everywhere, torn between hope of gain and dread of the bayonet; of armies dwindling to guerilla bands, each with more officers than common soldiers and each with its usual quota of visionaries and fanatics, of correct, conventional folk and mere adventurers, of honest fellows, ruffians, and sots. As for cruelty, well, the highly specialized Letts who served the Reds as hangmen had perfected the art of torture in a manner worthy of the most celebrated Mongol traditions. The "Chinese Hand," for example, was reserved especially for officers, because of their famed white gloves, although by that time gloves were only a memory for us all in the state of abject poverty and humiliation which we had accepted as our lot in common. To give you an idea of the lengths men will go in bar-

barous refinement, let us say no more than that the victim was slapped with the skin of his own hand stripped from him while he was alive. I could mention other details more atrocious still, but accounts of such nature vary between idle excitement and sadism. The worst examples of savage ferocity only harden the auditor that much more, and since the human heart has about as much softness as a stone anyhow I see no need for going further in that direction. Our men were certainly not lacking in invention either, but so far as I was concerned I preferred to deal out death without embellishment, as a rule. Cruelty is the luxury of those who have nothing to do, like drugs or racing stables. In the matter of love, too, I hold for perfection unadorned.

Furthermore, whatever the dangers an adventurer chooses to face (for an adventurer is what I have become), he seldom feels able to enter into the political animosities involved. Perhaps I am generalizing from a wholly individual case of moral impotency: of all the men that I know I am least disposed to seek out ideological incitements in order to love or hate my fellow beings; it is only for causes in which I do not believe that I have been willing to risk my life. My hostility to the Bolsheviks was a matter of caste, and that was natural enough at a time when the cards had been shuffled less often than at present, and by less clever tricks; but the plight of the White Russians, on the other hand, stirred me very little, and the future of Europe has never kept me awake nights. Once swept into the Baltic imbroglio I tried only to be a useful wheel in the whole machine, and to play as rarely as possible the rôle of crushed finger.

What else was left for a boy whose father had managed to get himself killed at Verdun, leaving for legacy only an Iron Cross and some debts, and a title good, at best, for catching an American wife? As for my mother, she was half lost in dreams; she passed her time reading Buddhist scripture, or the poems of Rabindranath Tagore. In my perpetually unsettled existence Conrad was at least a fixed point, a center, a heart. He was Balt with some Russian ancestry; I was Prussian with French and Baltic blood in my veins, so we cut across two neighboring nationalities. I had early discovered in him that same faculty which I myself alternately cultivated and restrained, of valuing nothing too high to be free to disdain it while tasting it to the full. But enough of these psychological explanations for what is only spontaneous accord between minds and temperaments, and bodies as well, not to mention that unexplained portion of flesh which has to be called the heart, whatever people may say, and which beat so admirably alike in us both, if somewhat less strongly in his breast than in mine. His father, in spite of sympathies on the German side, had died of typhus in a concentration camp on the outskirts of Dresden where some thousands of Russian prisoners were rotting away in vermin, and in their own melancholy. My father, though so proud of our French name and descent, had met his death in a trench of the Argonne Forest at the hands of an African soldier fighting for France. Too many such misapprehensions were to cure me forever after of holding ready-made convictions.

For us in 1915, happily, war and even bereavement impressed us chiefly in their aspect of summer vacation. We got out of lessons and examinations, and all the pother about children growing up. Kratovitsy was in a backwoods region of Kurland, near what used to be the old frontier between Russia and Germany in those days. Family ties and connections could sometimes serve as passports in that period when military discipline was already relaxing on the

Russian side. Although my mother was a Balt, and cousin to the Counts of Reval, she would not have been readmitted to the province by the Russian authorities because of her status as widow of a Prussian officer, but they were long willing to wink at the presence of a boy of sixteen. My youth gave me leave to stay with Conrad there in that lonely domain where I had been entrusted to the care of his aunt, a half-witted spinster who stood for the Russian part of the family, and to Michael the gardener, a perfect watch dog.

I remember our swims at dawn in the fresh lake water, or in the half-salt of the estuaries, where our feet left identical imprints on the sand, all quickly absorbed by the powerful suction of the sea. There were noonday rests in the hay where we discussed the problems of the time, chewing impartially at grass or tobacco, certain of doing far better than our elders and never suspecting that we were reserved only for other follies, and new catastrophes. In winter we skated together, or sometimes passed the short afternoons at that strange game of "Angels," where you lie with arms outspread to trace wings upon the snow. And then came the good nights of heavy slumber on Lettish farms, when the peasant wives, appalled but touched, too, by our boyish appetites in those times of food restrictions, gave the best featherbeds and the "great room" to their young guests.

There was no lack of girls, either, in that northern Eden isolated in the midst of war: Conrad would gladly have attached himself to their colorful skirts had I not treated all such fancies with scorn. He was one of those sensitive souls who are wounded to the quick by disdain, and who in all conscientiousness begin to doubt even their most cherished predilections the moment that a friend, or a mistress, perhaps, turns them to ridicule. In one respect there was a subtle but absolute difference between Conrad and me, like that between alabaster and marble. Conrad's susceptibility and softness were not merely a matter of age: his was one of those natures which receive and retain all impressions with the ease of an exquisite velvet. One could readily imagine him at thirty a docile civil servant, under the old Russian régime; or an officer in the Guards, trim and an expert horseman, but still boyishly shy; or turned humdrum country squire, pursuing farm girls, or boys; or even, in these post-war times, a poet cut to the pattern of T. S. Eliot or Jean Cocteau, and frequenting Berlin bars.

In any case, the differences between us were only in our moral fiber; in physical make-up we were alike, tall and limber and hardy, each with the same heavy tan and the same shade of blue in our eyes. Conrad's hair was fairer than mine, but no need to go into that. The country folk took us for brothers, a simple solution for those who have no conception of ardent friendship; when we protested, with strict regard for literal truth, they were willing at most to reduce so plausible a relationship by one degree, labelling us cousins. If now at times I happen to waste a night talking with café intellectuals of the despairing type (a night that might have been better spent in sleep or pleasure, or simply in solitude), I always astound them in saying that I have known happiness, the real thing, the inalterable gold piece exchangeable for whole handfuls of lesser coin, or for bundles of postwar marks, but nevertheless always retaining its substance unchanged, and untouched by devaluation. To have once possessed such happiness leaves one proof against vague philosophizing; it helps to simplify life, and life's opposite, as well. Whether that felicity emanated from Conrad or only from our youth itself I cannot say, but it hardly matters, since youth for me died with Conrad. So in spite of the difficulty of the times Kratovitsy was a kind of Paradise, vast and calm, without serpent or interdiction. Not even Aunt Prascovia with her frightful nervous tic disturbed us. As for the young girl, she did not count; she was careless about her attire, and did nothing but devour books lent to her by a young Jewish student at Riga; she had no use for boys.

But the time came when I had to slip over the border to report for military training; had I avoided it I should have failed to live up to what was, after all, most decent in me. I took my first drill under sergeants weakened from dysentery and hunger; their thoughts centered solely upon bread ration cards. Some of my drillmates were agreeable enough, and were already launched upon the wild freedom of the postwar era to come. Two months more and I should have been used to stop the gap which the Allied artillery had made in our ranks, and should at this very moment, perhaps, be peacefully amalgamated to French soil or its wines, or else to the blackberries growing along the French roads. But I arrived just in time to see certain defeat for our armies, and hollow victory for our opponents. The brave days of armistice, revolution, and inflation set in. I had lost everything, of course, and could look forward, with sixty million others, to a totally empty future.

I was just at the age to be caught by sentimental appeals in rightist or leftist doctrines, but I have never been able to swallow their noisome bait. As I have said already, I seek no pretext for any of my actions; human factors alone count for me, and my decisions have always turned upon some particular face or form. The conflagration in Russia was filling all Europe with a smoky haze of ideas which passed for new; Kratovitsy was serving as headquarters for a Russian army; communications between the Baltic countries and Germany were becoming precarious, but anyhow Conrad was not of the letter-writing type. I considered myself adult (that was my only youthful illusion), and, in any case, compared to those youngsters and the foolish old woman at Kratovitsy I was experience and maturity personified. I began to feel a sense of responsibility that was almost paternal, and my concern extended even to the young girl and the aunt.

A volunteer corps under Baron von Wirtz was already engaged against the Red army in Estonia and Kurland, and when I decided to enlist with him, too, my mother, in spite of her pacifist leanings, approved. The poor woman had property in those countries which was threatened by the Bolshevik advance, and her revenue from it, though steadily decreasing, was her sole guarantee against ending her days as a seamstress or shop attendant. But admitting all that, it is none the less true that the rise of communism in the East and inflation in Germany both proved timely in helping her to conceal from her friends that we were penniless, and had lost everything long before the Kaiser or Russia or France had dragged Europe into war. Better to appear the victim of general catastrophe than relict of a man whose pockets had been emptied by women in Paris, and by croupiers at Monte Carlo.

I had friends in Kurland and knew the country; I spoke the language, and even some local dialects. But in spite of my efforts to reach Kratovitsy as fast as possible it took me three months to get beyond Riga and bridge that distance of sixty miles. Three months of dank and foggy summer, buzzing with dealers from New York who had come to buy jewels at a profit from Russian refugees. Three months of army discipline, strict enough still, of abortive military operations and staff gossip, of dull anxieties throbbing sometimes like a toothache. In the eleventh week of this, Conrad turned up, as pale and elated as Orestes in the opening of Racine's play, and smartly outfitted in a uniform that must have cost his aunt one of her last diamonds; he had a small scar on his lip, like a dark violet. He had kept a certain child-like innocence and the gentleness of a young girl, along with that same dare-devil courage which he used to display when, like someone moving in a trance, he would leap on the back of a bull, or of a surging wave. His evenings were spent in scribbling verse, in feeble imitation of Rilke.

At the first glance I could see that his life had stood still in my absence; it was harder for me to admit that, in spite of appearances, the same had been true for me. Away from Conrad I had lived as if on a journey, but when he was there both mind and body could be at rest, reassured by such simplicity and frankness, and for that very reason were free to attend to whatever else had to be done. Everything about him made me trust him implicitly, as it has never been possible for me to do with anyone since that time. He was the ideal companion in war, just as he had been the ideal childhood friend. Friendship affords certitude above all, and that is what distinguishes it from love. It means respect, as well, and total acceptance of another being. That my friend repaid me to the last penny for the confidence and esteem which I had placed in him he proved to me by his death. In a setting less desolate than that of war and revolution his varied talents would have helped him to get along better than I: his verses would have been admired, and his beauty, too; he would have been a success in Paris with some patroness of the arts, or might have strayed into artistic cliques in Berlin. It was only for his sake, actually, that I ever got into that Baltic brew, where all the chances were against us; and it soon became apparent that he was staying in it only for me.

I learned through him that the Red occupation of Kratovitsy had been of short duration, with remarkably little damage, thanks perhaps to the presence there of young Gregory Loew, the Jewish clerk now turned lieutenant, absurdly enough, in the Bolshevik army; it was he who used to advise Sophie, in his obsequious way, on her reading, when he worked in a bookstore in Riga. Then the great house had been retaken by our own troops, but continued to be in full combat zone, exposed to surprise attacks and machine-gun fire. During the last alarm, Conrad said, the women had taken to the cellars, but Sonia —they persisted in using her Russian pet name—had refused to stay under cover and, in a fit of mad daring, had gone out to walk her dog.

The thought of our troops cantonned on the family estate disturbed me almost as much as the proximity of the Reds; the last resources of my friend would inevitably be drained dry. I was beginning to know what civil war meant to a partially disbanded army: those most apt to look out for themselves were sure to seek winter quarters in localities where supplies of wine and of girls were still relatively intact. That region was ruined by its protectors, not by revolution or war. Its fate meant little to me on the whole, but I cared about Kratovitsy, so pulled what strings I could. I urged the point that my knowledge of the topography and resources of the district could be put to use. After endless delay and postponements my superiors grasped what should have been obvious from the start; thanks to the helpful connivance of one or two persons, and the intelligent comprehension of a few others, I was finally sent to reorganize brigades of volunteers in the South-East section of the country.

A pitiable command it was, and we took it over, Conrad and I, in more pitiable condition still, all caked with mud past recognition even for the very dogs of Kratovitsy, who barked at our approach. We did not arrive till the last hour of the blackest of black nights. Doubtless proving my knowledge of topography, we had floundered till dawn in the marshes, hardly two paces from the Reds' advance posts. Our brothers in arms, who were still at table, rose to greet us, and helped us into dressing gowns which had been Conrad's in better days and were now generously restored to us ornamented with spots and riddled with holes from burning cigar ash. Aunt Prascovia's spasmodic twitching had grown worse in the recent commotion: her grimaces were enough to rout a whole enemy army. As for Sophie, she was no longer a lump of a girl; she had real beauty, and the fashion for short hair became her. But she seemed to be brooding; her lips had a bitter line; she read nothing now, and her eyenings were spent in savage poking at the drawing-room fire, sighing the while like a heroine in Ibsen utterly fed up with life.

But I am ahead of my story and should describe more exactly that moment of return, the door opened by Michael dressed half in livery thrown over his military breeches, his stable lantern lifted at arm's length in the entrance hall where chandeliers had so long gone unlighted. The white marble panels had the same glacial aspect as ever, as if someone had chosen a Louis XV style for the walls of an Eskimo dwelling. I shall never forget the expression on Conrad's face, touched and at the same time profoundly disgusted, when he came back to find the place just sufficiently intact that each minor damage struck him as an outrage, from the splintered star in the great stairway mirror to the fingermarks on the doorknobs. The two women were living at that time practically immured in a small sitting-room on the floor above, but the clear ring of Conrad's voice made them venture forth; I could see a fair, tousled head appearing at the top of the stairs. More gliding than running, Sophie sped down the balustrade base, her small dog yapping at her heels. She threw her arms first around her brother and then around me, laughing and dancing for joy:

"It's actually you? And you, too, Erick?"

"Present," answered Conrad. "No, it's the Prince of Trebizond!" He seized hold of his sister to waltz her around the hall, releasing her almost at once to rush towards a comrade. She came to a stop in front of me, flushed as after a ball:

"Erick! How you have changed!"

"Haven't I, though?" I rejoined. "Simply BEYOND recognition!"

"No," she shook her head.

"To the health of the prodigal brother!" young Franz von Aland sang out from the dining room door where he stood with a glass of brandy in hand. He began to chase after the girl, "Come now, Sophie, just a drop!"

"So you think you'll make a monkey of me, do you?" she retorted, and ducking under the young officer's arm as he reached out to catch her she escaped through the half-open door which led to the pantry, calling back, "I'm going to see that you get something to eat!"

Meanwhile Aunt Prascovia was still at the head of the stairs, leaning over the balustrade and gently daubing her tear-stained face. Cooing like some ailing old dove, she was attributing our salvation to her prayers in that bedroom fairly plastered with icons and reeking with candle-wax, and the scent of death. The smoke of her tapers had blackened the images, one of them very old. Its silver eyelids had once enclosed two fine emeralds, but during the brief occupation a Bolshevik soldier had made off with the gems, and from that time on Aunt Prascovia knelt at the feet of a blind protectress.

After a moment Michael came up from below stairs, carrying a platter of smoked fish. Conrad called for his sister in vain; Franz von Aland assured us, with a despairing shrug, that she would not reappear any more that night, so we supped without her. I saw her again the next morning in her brother's room, and there, too, each time she managed to slip out of sight as easily as young felines do in reverting to their natural state. Still, in the first excitement of our return she had kissed me warmly, and I could not help thinking, with a shade of melancholy, that that was my first kiss from a young girl, and that I had never had a sister. So of course, in so far as was possible, I made a sister of Sophie.

Life in the great house resumed its course in the intervals between the fighting. The only servants left to us were an aged housemaid and the gardener Michael; some Russian officers, escaped from Kronstadt, were crowded in upon us like guests at a dull hunting party that threatens to go on forever. Two or three times, when shots in the distance had awakened us, we tried to shorten the interminable night hours by playing three-handed bridge; to the dummy, our ghostly fourth, we could almost always give a name, even a familiar name, that of one of our men newly slain by an enemy bullet. Sophie's moodiness would melt in part, but her strange, wild grace remained; there are lands like that: they keep their wintry guise, even with spring's return. The pallor of her face and hands seemed to take on a luminous quality under the light of our lamp, prudently concentrated as it was. She was exactly my age, and that ought to have served me as warning, but in spite of her womanly form what struck me most was her aspect of injured adolescence. It was evident that something more than those two years of war had modified each feature of her face, leaving it both stubborn and tragically sombre. To be sure, at the age when she should have been going to her first balls she had had to endure the dangers of gun-fire and the horror of tales of execution and rape; she had known hunger at times, and at all times fearful anxiety. Her cousins in Riga had been lined up against the wall of their house by a Red squadron and shot; the effort she had made to adjust to a life so utterly different from her girlish dreams would have been enough in itself to account for the strained look in her eyes.

But either I am greatly mistaken, or Sophie was

not tender-hearted; she was only infinitely generous and warm; the symptoms of these two related maladies are often confounded. I could sense that something had happened which was more vital for her than national and international convulsion, and at last I was beginning to understand what those months must have been for a girl more or less alone among men continually excited by drink and by danger. Youths whom two years before she would have known, at most, only as correct dancing partners had been brutally quick to teach her the realities hidden beneath conventional love-talk, rapping at night on her bedroom door, pressing an arm about her waist while she struggled to free herself even if she tore her worn dress, already threadbare, or harmed her young breasts. . . . Here before me was a Sonia indignant at the slightest suspicion of desire, and everything in me which differentiates me from mere women-chasers, for whom any girl is a windfall, could not but approve her despair.

At last one morning I learned from Michael, as he dug potatoes in the park, the secret that everyone knew, but which our comrades had had the grace to keep quiet, and continued to keep so to the end, sc that Conrad never did know. Sophie had been raped by a Lithuanian sergeant (he was wounded soon after and evacuated to the rear). The fellow was drunk at the time, but came blubbering the next day to ask forgiveness, kneeling before her in the presence of some thirty persons in the great hall. That scene must have been even more sickening for the girl than the bad moments of the preceding day. She lived for weeks in the shock of the experience, and in the fear of being with child. Great as my intimacy was to be with Sophie thereafter, I never had the courage to allude to her tragic misadventure; the subject was always avoided between us, though always present.

And yet, strangely enough, my knowledge of that affair brought her closer to me. Had she been perfectly innocent or fully protected Sophie would only have bored and embarrassed me somewhat, as the daughters of my mother's friends in Berlin used to do; but now that she was sullied, her experience bordered upon my own, and the episode of the sergeant made a queer parallel with my unique and revolting visit to a brothel in Brussels.

Then distracted by new and greater suffering she seemed to forget the incident to which my thoughts always returned, and the intensity of that diversion for her is perhaps my only excuse for the torments I caused her. My presence and that of her brother gradually restored her to her rank as mistress of the great household at Kratovitsy, a position which she had so far lost as to be no more than a terrified prisoner in her own home. With what amounted, touchingly, almost to bravado she consented to preside at table and to give her hand, when the meal was over, to each officer to kiss. For a brief period her eyes regained their startling candour, which was simply the radiance of a royal soul; then they clouded over again, those all-revealing eyes, and I saw them glow with that strange limpidity but one time more, in circumstances which are only too much with me still.

Why is it that women fall in love with the very men who are destined otherwise, and who accordingly must repulse them, or else deny their own nature? After my return to Kratovitsy Sophie's deep blushes and sudden disappearances, her sidelong glances so little suited to her straightforward ways, all suggested to me no more at first than the natural confusion of a young girl naïvely attracted towards a newcomer. Later on, after being informed of her mishap, I learned to interpret less incorrectly those symptoms of mortal humiliation, which she exhibited in her brother's presence, too. But then, after that, I was too long content with this second explanation, right though it once had been, and all Kratovitsy was talking with sympathy or amusement of Sophie's passion for me while I was still holding to the myth of a terrified young girl.

Weeks passed before I realized that cheeks sometimes red, sometimes pale, a face and hands trembling but controlled, silences followed by a rush of words signified something other than shame, and even more than desire. I am not trying to boast of success with women; such a claim ill becomes a man who has no esteem for the sex, and who, as if to confirm himself in his opinion, has chosen to frequent only the worst of them. So I was bound to be mistaken about Sophie, and all the more that her voice, now brusque, now tender, her cropped hair, short smocks and heavy shoes perpetually encrusted with mud made her seem to me but a brother to her brother. I was wrong, of course, then saw my error; then came the day, at last, when in that same error I discovered the one substantial element of truth that I have ever encountered in my life. Meanwhile, to complicate matters further, my feeling for Sophie was just that sense of easy familiarity that a man has for boys who are of no special interest to him.

Such a false position was the more dangerous in that Sophie, though born the same week as I and under the same stars, was far from being the younger in misfortune; she was my elder in that respect. After a certain time it was she who led in the game, and she played all the more intently because her life was at stake. Besides, my attention was necessarily divided; not so, hers. For me there was Conrad and the war, and a few ambitions gone overboard since. Soon nothing counted for her but me alone, as if all human kind around us had been reduced to minor figures in the cast. It was simply in order to give me enough to eat that she helped the maidservant with kitchenwork and the poultry yard; when eventually she took a lover it was only to infuriate me. I was fated to lose, even if no joy were to ensue for her; I had need of all my powers of resistance against so ardent a being, for she gave herself utterly over to her one consuming thought.

Unlike most men of a reflective turn of mind, I

am not disposed to self-depreciation. Nor am I more given to self-praise. I feel too strongly that each of our actions is an absolute, a thing complete, necessary and inevitable, although unforeseen a moment before and past history the moment after. Involved in a series of decisions each final in itself, I had had no time to consider myself as a problem, no more than an animal does. But if adolescence is a period of inadaptability to the natural order of things I had certainly remained more of an adolescent and less adapted than I supposed, for the discovery of that simple fact of Sophie's love left me stunned and slightly scandalized. In the circumstances of my life at Kratovitsy, to be taken by surprise was to be in danger, and to be in danger meant to spring to attack. I ought to have hated Sophie; she never suspected how much it was to my credit that I did nothing of the sort. But those who are rejected in love retain one advantage: they have played rather cheaply upon our pride. Our own complacency, and our pleasure at being valued, at last, as each of us always hopes to be, work together to this result, and thus one yields to the temptation of playing God to one's adorer.

I must admit, too, that Sophie's infatuation was

less out of reason than may appear: after such a series of ordeals she was finally in contact again with someone of her own social background and childhood environment; all the novels that she had read from the age of twelve had steadily pointed out that friendship for a brother leads directly to love for the sister. Such a vague, instinctive calculation was right as far as it went; she could hardly be blamed, of course, for failing to reckon with one unforeseeable trait. I was fairly well born, rather good looking, and young enough to arouse all the usual expectations, so I seemed just made to fulfill the aspirations of an immature girl confined, up to that time, to the company of a few dull brutes of no consequence and the most seductive of brothers; nor had Nature seemed to endow her with the slightest inclination towards incest. But perhaps even incest figured here, for memory's magic transformed me, in her eyes, into an elder brother.

How could one not play, holding all the cards? If I passed at each turn that was playing, still. Between Sophie and me an intimacy swiftly sprang up like that between victim and executioner. The cruelty was not of my making; only the circumstances were to blame, but it is not so certain that the whole situation was not to my liking. Surely brothers are as blind as husbands, for Conrad suspected nothing. His was one of those natures steeped in dreams who by some happy instinct can disregard whatever is irritating or falsified around them, contenting themselves with plain facts of the night and the simple truths of day. Trusting in a kindred spirit, whose complexities he felt no desire to explore, he read, slept, ran the telegraph, risked his life, and continued to scribble verses which were no more than the feeblest reflection of the exquisite soul that he was. For some weeks Sophie went through all the agonies of a woman who supposes that her love has not been understood, and who is exasperated accordingly; then angered by what she took to be my stupidity she wearied of a situation which only romanticists would enjoy, for there was not a sentimental bone in her body. She made some avowals that were intended to be complete, but which were sublime in their understatement:

"How comfortable it is here!" she would exclaim, settling down in one of the park shelters during some brief interval that we managed to procure alone, by recourse to devices ordinarily employed only by lovers; and with a single skilfull motion she would scatter the ashes of the short peasant pipe that she liked to smoke.

"Yes, it *is* good," I would repeat after her, intoxicated by that wholly new feeling of tenderness, like a musical theme introduced in my life; and somewhat awkwardly I would touch her firm arms across from me on the garden table, much as I might have patted a horse or a fine dog recently acquired.

"Do you trust me?" she would ask.

" 'What heart so pure as yours,' my dear," I would quote to her in reply.

One day, leaning on her elbows and cupping her hands to support her chin, she began, "Erick, I'd rather tell you straight out that I've somehow come to love you . . . So, whenever you wish, do you understand? And even if it's not serious. . . ."

"With you, Sophie, everything is always serious."

"No," she protested, "you don't believe me." And tossing her willful head in a gesture of defiance more winning than any caress she added:

"Still, you need not imagine that I am so nice to everyone."

We were both too young to be entirely natural, but Sophie had a disconcerting honesty and directness which increased the chances for misunderstanding between us. Nothing but a pine table, still smelling of resin, separated me from this girl who was offering herself without further ado; though I kept on dotting indications in ink on the worn ordnance map before me, my hand grew less and less sure. As if to avoid the merest suspicion of trying to trap me Sophie had worn no rouge (such things came only later on), and had put on her oldest dress; she had chosen this hut with its poor wooden stools not far from the courtyard where Michael was splitting logs. At the very moment that she supposed herself to have been virtually lewd her ingenuousness would have delighted the average mother.

Such candour, however, surpassed the ablest strategy; if I had loved Sophie it would have been for just such a direct attack launched by one in whom I was still choosing to see the opposite of a woman. I beat a retreat with the help of the first pretexts that came to mind, feeling for the first time something ignoble in the true situation. To be perfectly clear, what was shameful in the matter was simply that I had to lie about it to Sophie.

From that moment on, the part of wisdom would have been to avoid the girl, but, aside from the difficulty of flight in our besieged state, I soon grew to depend upon the very alcohol which she afforded me, though I certainly never intended to abuse it. I admit that I deserve to be kicked for such self-indulgence, but while Sophie's feeling for me had raised my first doubts as to the legitimacy of my views on life, her unqualified offer of herself re-affirmed me in my dignity, or my vanity, as a man. What was ludicrous in the whole affair was this: it was my coldness and unresponsiveness that had won her; if in our first encounters she had seen in my eyes what she now sought there in vain she would have repulsed me with horror. Looking back upon what she had done, as scrupulous souls so readily do, she deemed herself lost by the daring of her avowal, for she little suspected that pride, too, can be gratified, as much as the body. Going next to the other extreme, she resolved upon restraint, like a woman of other days heroically tightening her corset: there was only a taut face before me, contracted to keep from trembling. This artless girl was suddenly acquiring the strange beauty of acrobats, and of martyrs: her valiant effort had raised her to the narrow pedestal of love without hope, reservation, or question, but she could hardly hold there for long.

Nothing moves me more than courage: so total a sacrifice deserved complete trust from me. But she never believed that I trusted her, since she did not suspect how much I distrusted others. In spite of appearances to the contrary, I do not regret having yielded to Sophie as much as it lay in my nature to do; at the first glance I had caught sight of something in her incorruptible, with which one could make a compact as sure, and as dangerous, as with an element itself. Fire may be trusted, provided one knows that its law is to burn, or to die.

I hope that our life side by side in Kratovitsy left Sophie with some memories as vivid as mine have been; that hardly matters, though, since she did not live long enough to treasure her past. By Michaelmas we had snow; then came a thaw, followed by new snowfalls. At night, with lights blacked out, the great house looked like an abandoned ship, locked in a belt of ice. Conrad would work alone in the tower while I concentrated upon the dispatches that always strewed my table; Sophie would come to my room, groping her way along like someone blind. She would sit on the edge of the bed, swinging legs encased half-way in coarse, thick woollen socks. Although she must have reproached herself severely for failing to keep to the terms of our silent accord, she could no more be other than a woman than a rose can be aught but a rose. Everything about her bespoke a desire involving the soul far more, even, than the body. The hours would wear on and conversation would languish, or turn to mild abuse; Sophie would invent pretexts to linger in my room; alone with me she unconsciously sought such occasions as amount to rape on the part of women. Exasperated as I was with it all, still I liked that kind of endless fencing, where my face kept its mask but hers was bare. The cold, airless room, fouled by the odor of a scantly fed stove, seemed transformed into a gymnasium where two young people, perpetually on their guard, were egging each other on in a match that would last until dawn. The first gleams of daylight would bring Conrad back, tired but content, like a boy coming home from school. Fellow officers ready to set out with me for the advance posts would look in through the doorway to suggest a drink, the first brandy of the day. Conrad might sit down by Sophie and teach her to whistle some bars of an English song, amidst roars of laughter; if sometimes her hands were trembling he would attribute the cause merely to drink.

I have often thought that Sophie was perhaps secretly relieved by my first refusal, and that her offer was made more for my sake, at the time, than for hers. She was still close enough to her one bad experience to approach physical love with more daring, but also with more fear, than do other women. Moreover, my Sophie was timid, and that explained her bursts of courage. She was too young to suspect that life is made up less of sudden exaltation and stubborn loyalty than of compromise, and remembrance betrayed. In that respect she would always have been too young, even had she lived to the age of sixty. Soon, however, she passed beyond the phase in which self-dedication is still an impassioned act of the will to reach a stage where total surrender is as natural as breathing to keep alive. From that time on I was the answer that she used to explain everything, and the fact of my previous absence seemed sufficient to her to account for her former misfortunes. She had suffered because no love had yet risen upon her horizon, and the lack of such light made harsher the way which the bad times had forced her to take. Now that love had come she was discarding one by one the last of her inhibitions, as simply as a wanderer chilled by rain sheds his wet garments in the sun; she stood before me more nude than woman has ever been on this earth. And possibly because she had spent all her fear and all her resistance to men in that single tragic encounter, thereafter she could offer to her first love only the ravishing sweetness of a fruit that is ripe for the cutting, or consuming.

Passion such as hers is all consent, asking little in return: I had merely to enter a room where she was to see her face take on that peaceful expression of one who is resting in bed. If I touched her I had the impression that all the blood in her veins was turning to honey. But the best of honeys will finally ferment: I little suspected that I was to pay hundredfold for each of my faults, and that Sophie's resignation in accepting them was to cost me higher still. Love had made her a glove in my hands, of a texture both supple and strong; when I left her and happened to come back some half-hour later I would find her in the same spot, like an object abandoned. I alternated between insolence and tenderness towards her, but that worked all to the same result, to make her love and suffer even more; my vanity compromised me with her exactly as desire would have done. Later on, when she began to mean more to me, I suppressed the tenderness. I was sure that Sophie would never tell anyone what she endured, but it seems to me strange even now that she did not make Conrad the confident of our rare joys. There must already have been a tacit complicity between us, since we agreed in treating Conrad like a child.

People always speak of classical tragedy as if it took place in a void, but actually it is conditioned by its setting. Our portion of good times and bad at Kratovitsy was set in scenes of corridors with boarded windows, where one was forever stumbling, and in the drawingroom, still unchanged, except for the loss of a panoply of Chinese arms to the Bolsheviks and a bayonet gash through a woman's portrait looking down on us from a panel above the door, as though the sitter were amused by the whole adventure. Time counted for us in this drama, too, in our impatient wait for the offensive, with death constantly at hand. For Sophie, life was reduced to its barest form: such allurements as other women owe to their dressing-tables, or to prolonged sessions with modistes and hairdressers, to that endless perspective of mirrors in lives so different, after all, from those of men (and often so much more protected), she seemed to come naturally by amid the trying promiscuities of a house converted into a barracks, in her mending of pink woollen underthings, as she had to do, before us under our lamp, in her washing of our shirts with a home-made soap that left her hands raw. The continual chafings of existence in state of alert left us bruised, but hardened, as well. I remember the day when Sophie took over the killing and plucking of two or three scrawny chickens for our meal: never have I seen so resolute a face so utterly free from cruelty; wisps of the down caught in her hair, and I blew them away, one by one; the sickly odor of blood clung to her hands. She used to come in from those sordid tasks weighed down by her tall snow boots, and would throw off her wet fur-lined jacket, refusing to eat, or perhaps on the contrary devouring the horrible pancakes which she still persisted in making for us from spoiled flour. On such a diet she grew thin.

Her zeal extended to us all, but still her smile was enough to tell me that these services were meant for me alone. She must have been genuinely kind, for she always let pass each occasion for causing me pain. Struggling with a type of defeat that women never forgive she did what all upright souls do when reduced to despair: she attributed to herself the worst of motives for her conduct, to berate herself further, and she judged herself as severely as Aunt Prascovia would have done, had Aunt Prascovia been capable of judgment. She supposed herself beneath contempt: such innocence as that should have been adored. Not for one second, however, did she dream of revoking what she had offered, a gift as final for her as if I had accepted. That was like her proud spirit: she was not one to take back the alms which a beggar refused. She may well have despised me, I know, and for her sake I hope that she did, but not all the scorn in the world could alter the fact that once in a rush of feeling she had kissed my hands. I watched eagerly for some sign of anger or well-deserved reproach, for any such action which she would have deemed sacrilege, but she always kept up to the standard of what I demanded of her absurd love. A fault of taste on her part in this matter of emotions would have reassured me, but disappointed me, as well.

She used to go with me in my inspections around the park; for her those walks must have been both Heaven and Hell. As for me, I liked the cold rain against our faces, plastering her hair down like mine; or the way she would stifle a cough in the palm of her hand, or absently twist a reed along the edge of the smooth, lonely pond, where one day there floated an enemy corpse. Suddenly she would plant herself against a tree, and for a brief interval I would let her speak of her love. One afternoon we were drenched to the skin and had to take refuge in the ruins of the hunting lodge; together in the one small room still graced with a roof we removed our wet clothes: I was making some show of bravado in treating this adversary as a friend. Sophie wrapped herself in a horseblanket and lighted a fire in order to dry my uniform and her own woollen dress. On the way home we had to drop low to the ground more than once to avoid bullets, and I put my arm around her, like a lover, to force her down beside me in a ditch, thus proving that all the same I did not wish her to die.

In the midst of all these torments for her I was irked to see hope perpetually, admirably rising in her eyes: there was something of that certitude in her that women have of their due, and that they keep to the point of death. Such touching incapacity for eternal despair seems to show that Catholic theory is right in placing more or less innocent souls in Purgatory, precipitating into Hell only those who have lost the power to hope. Of the two of us, she is the one whom people would have pitied, but actually she had the better part.

The terrible solitude of one who loves was increased for Sophie by the fact that she did not share the views of the rest of us: she had some sympathy for the Reds. For a nature like hers the supreme elegance evidently was to think that the enemy was right; accustomed to reasoning against herself she was probably as generous in justifying our opponents as she was in absolving me. These political inclinations dated from the time of her early girlhood; Conrad would have shared them had he not always promptly adopted my views on life. That

October was one of the most disastrous months of the civil war: almost completely abandoned by von Wirtz, who was confining his efforts strictly to the interior of the Baltic provinces, we held long councils, like ship-wrecked sailors, in the overseer's office for the estate.

Sophie attended these sessions, but stood braced against the frame of the door; she was doubtless struggling to maintain some kind of balance between personal convictions, which were, after all, the one thing she had of her own, and the comradeship in which she felt bound with us still. She must have wished more than once that a bomb would come to put an end to our futile staff meetings, and often her wish was very nearly fulfilled. In any case, there was so little tenderness in her make-up that she saw Red prisoners being executed below her very windows without one word of protest. I could feel that each of our resolutions passed in her presence provoked an explosion of violent resentment within her; yet in details of a practical nature she would give her opinion with the sound good sense of a peasant. When we were alone together we used to discuss the consequences of the war and the future of Marxism with a vehemence which showed that each of us needed an alibi for feelings still deeper within us. She did not conceal her political preferences from me; they were indeed the only thing about her that passion had not shaken.

Curious to see how far Sophie's subservience would go (a docility which was not servile because it was born of love), I tried more than once to prove her at variance with her principles, or rather with the ideas that Gregory Loew had implanted in her. But this was less easy to do than might have been expected; she would burst out with indignant protests. She seemed to feel obliged, strangely enough, to despise everything that I stood for, everything, that is, except me myself. Her confidence in me remained absolute, as before, and led her to make some further compromising avowals, along political lines this time, such as she would not have made to anyone else. One day I managed to make her carry some munitions up to our first line; I had thought that she might refuse, but she was only too eager to seize upon that chance to die. On the other hand, she never wished to join in our shooting expeditions; that was too bad, for already at the age of sixteen she had proved a remarkably accurate shot in the hunting season.

She wondered if she had rivals? Though such interrogations exasperated me they were probably made more out of curiosity than jealousy. Like an invalid who feels that his case is hopeless she was no longer seeking a remedy, but she still looked for causes for her ills. She insisted that I tell her the names of these women, and of course I was a fool to invent none. Once she assured me that she would readily have given way in favor of any woman that I loved, but little did she know herself: if such a rival had existed Sophie would have declared her unworthy of me, and would have tried to separate us. Some romantic fiction of a mistress left behind in Germany would scarcely have held up under pressure of our day-to-day intimacy and the opportunities which the nights afforded. And yet in a life so circumscribed as ours suspicion could point to only two or three creatures with too little to offer to serve as explanation, or to satisfy anyone. We had some absurd scenes on the subject of a red-headed peasant girl who came to bake our bread. It was on one of those occasions that I was brutal enough to tell Sophie that if I had wanted a woman she was the last I should have sought; and that was true, but the reason was not that she lacked beauty.

Woman-like, however, she thought only of that; she reeled like a barmaid under a drunkard's blow, then ran out of the room and up the stairs, holding fast to the balustrade; I could hear her stumbling and sobbing every step of the way.

She must have passed that night before the white-framed mirror of her schoolgirl bedroom, wondering if it were true that her face and body could appeal only to tipsy sergeants, and if her eyes, lips, and hair did ill-service to the love which she bore in her heart. In the glass were reflected the eyes of a child, or of an angel, perhaps; the face was broad with contours not sharply defined, like earth itself in spring, a region of fields gently sloping, traversed by streams of tears; the cheeks had the tint of sunlight on snow and the lips' pale rose almost made one tremble; her hair was as blond as those light golden loaves of good bread that we saw no more. But she despised all those features; they seemed to betray her, having no value for the man she loved; so, comparing herself with despair to Pearl White and the Empress of Russia, whose photographs hung on her wall, she wept until dawn, as she could do at twenty without disaster to the beauty of her eyes. The next day I observed that for the first time she had not put her hair up in curlers (on nights of alarm the things made her look like Medusa, serpent-crowned); accepting plainness once for all she heroically consented to appear before me with straight hair. I praised that smooth headdress, and, as I had foreseen, she took courage anew; but what concern she still had for her supposed lack of charm served only to give her some further assurance, as if now freed from all danger of allurement she felt all the more entitled to be considered as my friend.

I went to Riga to discuss the plans for the next offensive; two comrades went with me in the fitful old Ford, a specimen for American films. Kratovitsy was to be the base of those operations, so Conrad stayed at home to speed up our preparations with that particular capacity of his for combining activity with easy unconcern; I have never seen that quality in anyone else, but it reassured our men. He would, in fact, have been an admirable aide-de-camp (one of those ideal disciples without whom no master can be explained) had all the dreams of the future been realized, and had I become the young Bonaparte that I once hoped to be. Skidding along for two hours on icy roads we exposed ourselves to every variety of death that tourists risk on a Christmas vacation in Switzerland. The turn which things had taken, both in the war and in my personal affairs, exasperated me. My part in the anti-Bolshevik defence in Kurland meant more than danger of death: the truth is that records and accounts, responsibility for the sick, the telegraph, and the burdensome or even insidious presence of our comrades were all slowly undermining my relations with my friend. Human affection requires some degree of privacy around it, and a minimum of calm even in the midst of insecurity; neither love nor friendship is readily advanced in barracks rooms between stretches of mere fatigue duty. That was just what life at Kratovitsy had become for me, revolting fatigue duty, contrary to all expectation. Sophie alone was holding her own in that atmosphere of pernicious, deadly monotony; naturally enough, misery withstands damnable aggravations better than joy can do.

But it was simply to escape Sophie that I had gone myself on the Riga assignment. The city was more lugubrious than ever at that time of year, nearly November. I remember only our irritation at von Wirtz's hesitation and delays, and the vile champagne in a Russian night club. We had some drinks there with an unpretentious little Jewess from Moscow and two Hungarian girls who were posing as French, but whose Parisian accent was enough to set my teeth on edge. Months had passed since I had left styles and fashions behind me; it was hard to get used to the ridiculous, pot-shaped hats that covered the women's eyes.

Towards four in the morning I came to in a room of the one fairly good hotel left in Riga, in company with one of the Hungarians; my mind was just clear enough for me to say to myself that I should have preferred the Jewish girl all the same. I may as well admit that such conformity to common practice was chiefly due to my attempt to go along with the others, but was also in small part a challenge to my own lack of inclination; the greatest self-constraint, as you well know, is not always employed in trying to walk in virtue's path. One's motives are so mixed and confused, anyhow, that at this distance from that whole affair I cannot say whether I hoped to come nearer to Sophie in that way, indirectly, or simply to insult her by likening her desire, which I knew to be the purest conceivable, to a half-hour passed in a disordered bed with the first woman who offered. Some of my disgust would inevitably rebound upon Sophie; perhaps I was beginning to need fortifying in my specific aversion. There is no denying that my fear of getting too deeply involved, low as it was, contributed to the caution of my attitude towards the young girl; I have always dreaded committing myself, and with a love-stricken woman how can one fail to commit oneself?

At least that humble café singer from Budapest had no aspiration to encumber my future. It must be admitted, however, that she clung to me during those four days at Riga with the tenacity of an octopus; her long fingers in their white gloves made me think of those creatures. In hearts like hers, open to all comers, there is always a special place ready, under a rose lamp-shade, where such women try desperately to install the first likely man. I left Riga with a kind of sullen satisfaction in telling myself that I had nothing in common with those people or that country, or even that war; no more, in fact, than with those rare pleasures invented by man to distract him from life itself. Thinking for the first time of the morrow, I considered emigrating to Canada with Conrad and living on a farm near the Great Lakes, all without the slightest reflection that in such vague projects I was disregarding many of my friend's chief interests.

Conrad and his sister were waiting for me outside, on the entrance staircase; the marquise under which they stood had lost all its panes of glass, shattered by vibration from artillery fire the summer before; only the lead framework was left, like a great dead leaf stripped to the veins. Rain was trickling through, so Sophie had tied a kerchief over her head, peasant-fashion. The two of them were worn out from duties attended to during my absence: Conrad was both flushed and pale, and my concern for his health, which was no longer strong, made me forget about everything else that evening. Sophie had ordered one of the last bottles of French wine brought up for us from the cellar where it was hidden. My two companions on that mission unbuttoned their long coats and sat down to supper, exchanging pleasantries on what had been for them the gay times in Riga; Conrad's eyebrows rose in polite, amused surprise. He had tried such dismal evenings as that with me, when one goes deliberately counter to one's inclinations, so another Hungarian girl or two was hardly news to him. As for

Sophie, she had spilled a little of the burgundy in trying to fill my glass, and she bit at her lip in noticing what she had done. She left the room to fetch a sponge, and worked as hard to obliterate the spot as if it had been the trace of some crime.

I had brought back some books from Riga; that night as I read under a lamp-shade improvised from one of our towels, I looked over at Conrad, fast asleep like a child in the adjoining bed, undisturbed by Aunt Prascovia's footsteps overhead; night and day she walked back and forth on the floor above us, still mumbling the prayers to which she supposed our relative safety was due. Of the two, brother and sister, it was Conrad, paradoxically enough, who answered more to the usual conception of a young girl descended from princely lineage. Sophie's wind-burned neck and her chapped hands, as she squeezed the sponge, had suddenly reminded me of the young farmhand Karl who used to curry our ponies when we were small. After my Hungarian friend, whose face was so creamed, massaged, and powdered, Sophie was ill-groomed, but beyond compare.

The fling at Riga hurt Sophie's feelings, but hardly surprised her; for the first time my conduct was something like what she had expected. Our intimacy was not diminished thereby; on the contrary, it increased; such ill-defined relationships are, in any case, strangely enduring. We were alarmingly frank towards each other, but you have to bear in mind that the fashion of the time put a premium upon utter sincerity. Instead of love-talk we talked *about* love, using mere words to soothe an anxiety which any other man would have quelled by caresses, or would simply have escaped by flight, an alternative which the circumstances did not permit. Sophie spoke freely of her one experience in love, though without ever mentioning that it had been wholly involuntary. On my side I concealed nothing, except the essential point. The unsophisticated girl followed my tales of whoredom with almost absurd attention, puzzling her brows. I believe that she began to take lovers only in order to attain in my eyes to that degree of seduction which she supposed street walkers to have. There is so little basic difference between total innocence and complete degradation that she fell at once to that level of cheap sensuality which she sought in order to please me: a transformation took place under my very eyes that was more startling than anything on a stage, and almost as conventional.

The change consisted at first only of details, almost pathetic in their naïveté: she managed to get some cosmetics, and discovered for herself the virtues of silk hose. Cheekbones heightened with rouge and eyes smudged with mascara (though fatigue had shadowed them enough already) were repellent to me, but of course I was as much to blame for all that as if I had disfigured her face with actual blows: those lips once exquisitely pale were not lying so much, after all, in striving to appear as if bleeding. More than one youth, Franz von Aland among others, tried to capture this fine butterfly, who was being consumed before their eyes by some inexplicable flame. Even I, the more seduced from the moment that others were attracted, and wrongly attributing my hesitations to scruple, came now to the point of regretting that Sophie was sister to the one being, precisely, to whom I felt myself bound by a kind of pact. But had she not possessed the only eyes in the world that counted for me I should not have looked at her twice.

Women's instinctive reactions in love are so limited in number and kind that it takes no astrologer's art to predict their course: this erstwhile tomboy was following the time-worn track of heroines of tragedy, seeking any diversion in order to forget. Intimate talks and exchanges of smiles, wild dancing to the music of a rasping gramophone, dangerous strolls in the firing zone all were resumed with boys more disposed to profit from them than I. First to benefit from this phase (as inevitable in women thwarted in love as the high agitation in initial stages of paresis) was Franz von Aland. He had fallen almost as abjectly in love with Sophie as the poor girl had done with me, and was only too happy to serve her as second choice; his ambitions had hardly aspired even that high. When he was alone with me he seemed always on the verge of offering some humble apology, such as excursionists make who have ventured upon a private road. Sophie must have taken vengeance upon him and me, and herself, as well, in discoursing to him incessantly about our love. Franz's meek submission was not conducive to winning me over to the notion of happiness with women. I still remember with something like pity that the slightest favor that Sophie accorded him, whether out of disdain, exasperation, or sheer promiscuousness, was like sugar to a dog.

In his short lifetime this ill-starred youth had managed to run into every kind of trouble, ranging from expulsion in his schooldays, for a theft that he had not committed, to the loss of his parents in 1917, assassinated by the Bolsheviks; even an operation for appendicitis had proved nearly fatal in his case. After a few weeks of comparative happiness with Sophie he managed to get taken prisoner; his body was found with a charred wound round the neck that meant torture from a slow-burning wick. Sophie learned this piece of news from me, told with as little gruesome detail as possible, and I was not displeased to see that the horrible ending was only one more tragedy for her, added to so many others, and not a personal grief.

Then came further affairs with men, arising from that same need to silence, if only for a moment, the unbearable love monologue going on within her; but after a few awkward embraces these ventures were shamefacedly broken off, because she could no more forget than before. The most obnoxious of these vague passersby was, to my mind, a certain Russian officer, escaped from a Bolshevik prison, who spent eight days with us before leaving for Sweden on some hazy, improbable mission to one of the Grand Dukes there. From the very first evening I was treated to enough bragging about women from this drunkard, complete with amorous detail, to let me imagine only too well what was going on between Sophie and him on the leather couch of the gardener's cottage. I could not have endured sight of the girl thereafter had I read in her face, even once, anything that looked like joy. But she told me everything; she still touched me with those slight, discouraged gestures which were less a caress than the motion of someone blind, and each morning I beheld a woman reduced to despair because the man she loved was not the one with whom she had just been sleeping.

One evening, a month or so after my return from Riga, I was at work in the tower with Conrad; he was doing his utmost, I remember, to smoke a long German pipe. I had just come back from the village where our men were trying to reinforce our mud trenches as well as they could with pine saplings; it was one of those nights of thick fog, the safest of all, when hostilities were broken off on both sides because of "non-visibility of the enemy." My outer jacket, soaked through, was steaming at the stove which Conrad kept feeding with wretched little damp logs; he sacrificed them one by one with the regretful sigh of a poet who sees his trees burned for fuel. Sergeant Chopin entered with a message for me; from the doorway he signalled to me over Conrad's bent head, and his face was flushed and disturbed. I followed him to the stair landing. Chopin was son to the Polish overseer of the last Count of Reval, and in civilian life worked in a bank in Warsaw; he had a wife and two children, and was blessed with some good common sense. He fairly worshipped Conrad and his sister, and they, in their turn, looked upon him as a foster-brother. As soon as the Revolution began he had come back to Kratovitsy, and from that time on played the rôle of faithful friend in our little drama. He whispered to me that in crossing the underground rooms he had found Sophie completely drunk at the great table of the kitchens, which were always deserted at that hour; in spite of his urging (inept, no doubt) he had failed to persuade the young girl to go back upstairs to her room.

"That's how it is, Sir," he exclaimed to me. (He still addressed me as *Sir.*) "Think how ashamed she will be tomorrow if anyone sees her in such a state. . . ."

The good fellow still believed in Sophie's innate modesty, and curiously enough he was not wrong. I went down the winding back stairs, trying to keep my poorly oiled boots from squeaking on every tread. On that night of virtual truce not a soul was about at Kratovitsy: a muffled sound of snoring rose from the great hall of the second floor, where thirty exhausted lads lay dead to the world. Sophie was sitting in the kitchen at the scoured wooden table, balancing foolishly on a chair, the feet of which tilted unevenly so that the back made an alarming angle with the floor. Her legs sprawling before me, encased now in caramel-colored silk, were less those of a young goddess than of a young god. A bottle with a little brandy still in it swung from one hand hanging limply down.

The poor girl was unbelievably drunk; in the light of the stove a mottling of red spots showed on her face. I touched her shoulder, but for the first time she failed to give that appalling but exquisite shudder, like a wounded bird, under my hands; the euphoria induced by brandy had left her immune to love. She turned a vacant countenance towards me and spoke in a voice as befuddled as her eyes:

"Go and say 'Goodnight' to Texas, Erick. He is lying in the pantry."

I struck my cigarette lighter to guide my way in that storecloset where one stumbled on toppled piles of half-spoiled potatoes. The absurd little dog lay under the hood broken off from a discarded baby-carriage; I was to learn afterwards that he had found a hand grenade buried in the park, and had tried to root it out with the tip of his black muzzle, as if it were a truffle. The explosion reduced him to a pulp, of course; he looked like any cur crushed by a tram car in city traffic. I picked up the repulsive bundle gingerly, took a spade, and went out to dig a hole in the courtyard. The surface of the ground had been thawed by rain, so I buried Texas in the very mud which he so loved to roll in during his lifetime. When I got back to the kitchen Sophie was just draining off the last drop of brandy; she tossed the bottle into the coals, where the glass popped with a dull, muted sound, then raised herself unsteadily, leaning upon my shoulder for support and murmuring thickly,

"Poor Texas. . . . It's too bad, all the same. He was the only one who loved me. . . ."

Her breath reeked with the odor of alcohol. On reaching the staircase her legs failed her entirely, and I held her by both arms as she vomited her way up the steps; it was like leading a seasick passenger to her cabin. Once back in her small, disordered room she collapsed into an armchair while I set to work opening her bed. Her hands and feet were as cold as ice. I piled the covers upon her, and added a coat as well. Raised on one elbow she went on vomiting without knowing what she did, open-mouthed like some statue of a fountain. At last she sank back flat in bed, inert and moist as a corpse; her damp hair stuck to her cheeks like the marks of long, fair scars. I could hardly feel her pulse, so weak it was, though racing wildly.

Somewhere within her she must have kept that peculiar clarity of perception which is common to drunkenness, bewilderment, and terror, for she told me afterwards of feeling throughout that night sensations of swift descent as by sleigh or toboggan, the same sudden lurching and cold, the roaring of the wind, and of the arteries, the impression of being carried full speed towards a precipice no longer feared. I well know that feeling of fatal speed that alcohol gives to a flagging heart.

Sophie always supposed that my Good Samaritan vigil beside her badly soiled bed had left me one of the most sordid memories of my life. I should not have been able to explain to her that I was less uneasy than usual in her presence, that her pallor, the danger she was in, the spots and stains, and her abandon freer than in love itself were reassuring to me and rather beautiful; for her body lying so heavily on the bed reminded me of comrades attended in the same sorry state, and of Conrad himself. . . . I have forgotten to mention that in taking off her clothes I had noticed a long scar from a knife-thrust beside the left breast; the wound had evidently not been very deep. She admitted to me thereafter of an ill-planned attempt at suicide. Did it date from my time, or from that of the Lithuanian satyr? The fact is that I never could know, so I might as well not invent.

Sergeant Chopin had been right: Sophie was as chagrinned after this incident as a schoolgirl who has taken too much champagne at a wedding banquet. For a few days I reaped the benefit of a friend grown sadly reasonable, whose every look seemed to thank me, or to ask my pardon. There were some cases of typhus in the barracks; she persisted in nursing them and neither Conrad nor I could prevent her; I finally let the mad girl go ahead, decided as she seemed to be to die under my very eyes. In less than a week she was down in bed and was thought to have typhus, too, but she was only suffering from exhaustion and discouragement, from the strain of a love which was always changing form, like a nervous disorder which daily presents some new symptom; and from sheer unhappiness and dissipation combined.

It was now my turn to go to her room each morning in the small hours of dawn. The whole household took us for lovers, and that flattered her, I suppose, while arranging matters for me, also. I inquired after her health with the solicitude of a family physician; seated upon her bed I was absurdly fraternal. Had my kindness been deliberately calculated to wound Sophie more it could not have succeeded more completely. Sitting with her knees drawn up under the covers and resting her chin in her two hands, she gazed on me astonished, her eyes constantly filling with tears. The time had passed when she might have relished with good conscience such tender glances on my part, or such caresses as stroking her hair. Remembrance of the promiscuous meetings of the recent weeks made her wish to flee wherever she could outside herself, a feeling familiar to all wretches unable to bear with themselves any longer.

She strove to rise from her bed like one about to die. I made her lie down again, tucking her in between the rumpled sheets, though I knew that she would toss desperately there after I left. If to soothe her remorse I made light of those physical diversions as of no great importance I only inflicted a cutting blow to her self-esteem; and to something deeper and more essential still, to that undefined respect which a body has for itself. In the light of such new indulgence on my part, my former hardness and refusals, and even my smiles, seemed now to her like a trial the import of which she had not fully grasped, or an examination which she had failed to pass. Like an exhausted swimmer, she saw herself sinking within two strokes of shore at the very time when perhaps I might have begun to love her. If I had taken her to me then she would have wept with horror at the thought that she had lacked courage to wait. She suffered all the torments of an unfaithful wife punished with kindness, and such despair was only intensified by the rare moments of clear-sightedness when she recalled that, after all, she had no obligation to conserve herself for me. And nevertheless, anger and disgust, pity and irony, some vague regret on my part, and on hers a growing resentment, in sum, all our contrasting feelings bound us together like two lovers, or two partners in a dance. That much-desired bond did actually exist between us, and for my Sophie the worst torture of all must have been to feel how suffocatingly close it was, and at the same time how slight.

One night (for after all, most of my memories of Sophie are nocturnal except the last, which has the wan coloring of dawn), on a night, then, of aerial bombardment I noticed a square of light outlined on Sophie's balcony. Air attacks had been rare until then in our swamp-bird warfare; it was the first time at Kratovitsy that death was falling on us from the sky. That Sophie should deliberately call down danger, not only upon herself but upon her family and all the rest of us, was unthinkable. She had a room in the right wing, on the third floor. Her door was closed, but not locked; she was sitting at her table, within the circle of light cast by a large oil lamp that hung from the ceiling. The open casement window framed a landscape sharply defined by the cold winter night without. My struggle to close her shutters, swollen by the recent autumn rains, reminded me of stormy evenings in my childhood and the rush to barricade all windows in the mountain resort hotels. Sophie watched me glumly. At length she addressed me:

"Erick, would it bother you much if I died?"

I detested those dulcet, throaty inflections that she had adopted since she had begun to play the whore. The crash of a bomb spared me the need for reply; it sounded to the East, near the pond, and that made me hope that the storm was moving farther away. The next morning I learned that the shell had fallen just at the water's edge; for some days thereafter broken rushes floated on the surface, together with the upturned bellies of dead fish and the wreckage of a battered rowboat.

"Yes," she continued slowly, in the tone of one who is trying to grasp a situation, "I'm afraid, and that's odd when I come to think of it. Because it shouldn't really matter to me, should it?"

"As you please, Sophie," was my irritable response, "but that poor old woman is only one room away from yours. And Conrad. . . ."

"Oh, Conrad," she echoed, with a note of infinite weariness in her voice, and with such apparent indifference to her brother's fate that I wondered if she had begun to loathe him. But she had simply reached that state of utter exhaustion where nothing counted any more, and she had ceased to worry about the safety of those nearest to her, just as she had ceased to look to Lenin as a leader. She got up, uncertainly, holding on to the table with both hands, like an invalid hesitating to quit his armchair.

"Often," she said, coming closer to me, "it seems to me wicked not to be afraid. But if I were happy," and her voice had again become husky and tender, like a cello's deep tones, moving me, after all, in spite of myself, "maybe death wouldn't matter any more. Only two minutes of happiness, that would be like a last blessing sent from God himself. Are *you* happy, Erick?"

"Yes, I suppose so," I answered half-heartedly, suddenly realizing that what I was saying was a mere lie.

"I see. Only you don't look much like it," she rejoined in the teasing manner that suggested the schoolgirl of earlier days. "And it's because you are happy that you don't give a hang if you die?"

With her mended black shawl thrown over her childish flannel nightgown she looked for all the world like some young housemaid only half awakened by a midnight bell. I shall never know why I did anything so idiotic and uncalled for as to open the window again. The felling of trees so deplored by Conrad had cleared the land all the way to the river where, as every night, intermittent and ineffectual shots were being exchanged. The enemy plane was still circling above in the greenish sky; the air was filled with the hideous hum of its motor, as if all space were only a room where a giant wasp flew blindly about. I drew Sophie out on the balcony, as a lover might do on a moonlight night; together we watched the broad reflection of the lamp swaying ever so slightly on the snow below us. There must not have been much wind, for the patch of light barely moved. With my arm around Sophie's waist I had the feeling of testing her heart-beat: that overtaxed organ faltered, then started again, regaining a rhythm which was that of courage itself, and my one thought, as far as I can now recall, was that if we were to die that night, then I had chosen, after all, to die at her side.

Suddenly there was a terrific crash very close by; Sophie stopped her ears as if the din were more hideous even than death. The shell had fallen this time less than a stone's throw away, on the corrugated iron roof of the stable; that night two of our horses answered for us. In the incredible stillness that followed we could still hear the sound of a brick wall in halting collapse, and the horrible neighing of a dying horse. Behind us the window pane had shattered to bits; on stepping back into the room we trod upon broken glass. I put out the lamp, much as one lights it again after having loved.

She followed me into the corridor. A diminutive vigil light still burned there, unseen from outside, below one of Aunt Prascovia's icons. Sophie was breathing fast; her face was radiantly pale, which showed that she had understood me. I have lived through even more tragic moments with her, but none more solemn, or more like an exchange of vows. The turning point for her in my life, as I look back on it, was certainly that hour. As she raised her arms to me, I remember, her hands were marked with rust from the balcony where we had just been leaning; she fell on my breast as if she were reeling from a wound.

Most amazing of all, I accepted this gesture which she had taken nearly ten weeks to bring herself to. Now that she is dead, and that I have ceased to believe in miracles, I am glad that I kissed her lips one time, at least, and her wild hair. If she were to remain like a vast country subdued by me but never possessed, I was to remember, in any case, the exact taste of her very mouth that night, and the warmth of her living flesh. And if ever I could have loved Sophie utterly and simply with body and soul it was surely at that moment when we both were innocent as beings just resurrected. She was fairly throbbing against me, and no previous feminine encounter, whether with a chance pick-up, or with an avowed prostitute, had prepared me for that sudden, terrifying sweetness. Her body so yielding, yet rigid with delight, weighed in my arms almost as mysteriously as earth itself would have done had I entered some few hours before into death. I hardly know at what moment ecstasy changed into horror, releasing in me the memory of that starfish that Mother once forced into my hand on the beach at Scheveningen, almost provoking convulsions in me, to the consternation of the bathers. I wrenched myself from Sophie with a violence that must have seemed cruel to a body robbed of defence by felicity itself. She re-opened her eyes (they had closed) and read in my aspect something harder to bear, doubtless, than hatred or terror, for she recoiled, covering her face with her upraised arm, like a child who is slapped, and that was the last time that I ever saw her actually cry.

I had two other meetings alone with Sophie before everything was over. But from that evening on, whatever happened, it was as if one of the two of us were already dead, I in what concerned her, or she in that part of herself which had ventured to hope because she loved me.

The successive phases of love follow a monotonous course; what they still seem to me to resemble the most are the endless but sublime repetitions and returns in Beethoven's Quartets. During those dark weeks of Advent (for Aunt Prascovia, increasing her days of fast, kept us constantly in mind of the Church calendar), life went on among us with its usual percentage of annoyances, privations, and catastrophes. I witnessed or learned of the death of some of my few close friends in the fray; Conrad was slightly wounded; the village was taken and recaptured three times, so nothing was left of it but some sections of wall crumbling away under the snow. As for Sophie, she was calm, firm, helpful in many ways, but on the whole resistant. It was at about this time that Volkmar took up his winter quarters at Kratovitsy, together with the remnants of a regiment sent to us by von Wirtz. Since the death of Franz von Aland our small expeditionary force, made up of Germans, had been decreasing from day to day, and had been replaced by a mixture of Baltic and White Russian elements.

I had known this fellow Volkmar long enough to have detested him at the age of fifteen, when we went three times a week to the same mathematics tutor during the winter months passed at Riga. He resembled me about as much as a caricature resembles its original model: he was correct, dry, ambitious, and out for gain. He belonged to that type of men who though stupid are born to success, and who consider any new factor only in relation to their personal profit; such men base their calculations on the constants in life. Had there been no war he would have had not one chance with Sophie; he did not let this occasion slip. I was well aware that a woman isolated in the midst of a barracks acquires a prestige in the eyes of the men such as exists only for heroines of comic opera or tragedy. She and I had been considered lovers, a supposition false in the literal sense; but within a fortnight everyone was dubbing her and Volkmar engaged. Her half-somnambulistic interludes with boys who could afford her only a few moments of oblivion, if even that, could be endured, but the liaison with Volkmar upset me because she hid it from me. Not that she falsified anything; she simply withdrew all my rights in her life. To be sure, I was less to blame with regard to her by that time than I had been at the beginning of our relations, but one is always punished out of season.

Sophie was generous, however; she was still affectionate and considerate to me, the more so, perhaps, that she was beginning to judge me. So I failed to see that her love was coming to an end, just as I had failed to see its start. There are times when I still think that she loved me to the last, but naturally I mistrust an opinion so gratifying to my pride. She was sound enough, after all, to recover from more than one love affair: sometimes I imagine her married to Volkmar, mistress of a household with a family of children, and visibly stouter at middle age, squeezed into a tight-fitting girdle. But what makes such a view untenable is that my Sophie died in the same atmosphere and under the same stormy skies as had fostered our love. So in a way, and as the saying went at the time, I have the impression of having "won the war." To use a less odious expression, shall I say simply that I had been more clear-sighted in my deductions than Volkmar had been in his scheming, and that there certainly was an affinity between Sophie's nature and mine. But during that Christmas week Volkmar held all the trumps.

Occasionally I still knocked at her door at night, merely to humiliate myself with the assurance that she was not alone. There was a time, that is to say, a month earlier, when Sophie under the same circumstances would have laughed, falsely and enticingly, and that would have reassured me almost as much as if she had wept; but now these two would open the door, and the cool circumspection of the scene was in sharp contrast to the disorder of old, when underclothes and liquor bottles were always scattered about. Volkmar would proffer his cigarette case with due formality. What I can least endure is an effort to spare me, so I would go back where I had come from, imagining the while the whispering and vapid kissing resumed after I left. They were talking about me, in any case; I could be sure of that. Volkmar and I despised each other so heartily that sometimes I wonder if he had not singled Sophie out simply because all Kratovitsy had coupled us together. But I certainly must have cared for the girl far more than I had supposed, since it was so hard for me to admit that that pompous ass dared to love her.

I have never seen a gayer Christmas Eve than at Kratovitsy during that wartime winter. Conrad's and Sophie's absurd preparations annoyed me, so I made myself scarce on the pretence of having to write a report. Towards midnight, hunger and curiosity, as well as the noise of laughter and the scratching sound of one of my favorite records all got the better of me, so I went down to the drawing room where the dancers were circling in the light of an open fire and some twenty lamps assembled from different parts of the house. Once again I had the feeling of taking no part in others' pleasures, and voluntarily so, but the bitterness was not the less for that. On one of the heavily gilded console tables a supper of smoked raw ham, apples, and whisky had been set out; Sophie had baked the bread herself.

Paul Rugen's massive square shoulders kept me from seeing half the room; this giant of a doctor was sitting with his plate on his knees, rapidly putting away his portion of the viands, hurrying as always to get back to his hospital installed in Prince Peter's old stables. If Sophie had chosen this fellow, and not Volkmar, I should have forgiven her. Chopin, whose taste for parlor games nobody shared, was struggling to erect some structure from matches stuck into the neck of a broken bottle. Conrad, with his usual clumsiness, had cut his finger in trying to portion out the ham in very thin slices, and was using a handkerchief for bandage; the resulting silhouette helped him to vary the shadows which he was designing with his hands on the opposite wall. He was pale, and still limped from his recent wound. From time to time he would pause in his gesticulations to restock the gramophone.

La Paloma had given way to some whining novelty or other; Sophie was changing partners with every dance. After all, dancing was what she did best: she could glide like a swan, sway like a flower, and twirl like a flame. She was wearing her blue tulle gown in the style of 1914, the one ball dress she ever owned in her life; and even so, to my knowledge, she wore it only twice. That gown, both new and old-fashioned as it was, sufficed to change our erstwhile comrade into a heroine of romance. A host of young girls in blue tulle (in the mirrors) being the only other feminine guests at the party, the rest of the lads had to form couples between themselves. That very morning Conrad, in spite of his bad leg, had insisted upon climbing high in an oak tree to gather a bunch of mistletoe; such impish imprudence had provoked the first of the only two quarrels that I ever had with him. The idea about the mistletoe had come from Volkmar; hung from the darkened chandelier which none of us had seen alight since the days of our childhood it served the boys as pretext for kissing their girl partner. Each of these youths in turn pressed his lips to Sophie's, and she was haughty or amused, condescending or friendly, or sometimes even tender in her response.

When I came into the room Volkmar's turn had come; she exchanged a kiss with him which I knew full well to be different from anything inspired by love, but which left no doubt that it signified gay and confident accord. Conrad's greeting, "Well, Erick, everyone's here but you!" made Sophie turn her head. I stayed in the doorway, far from all the lights, on the side towards the music room. Sophie was near-sighted, but she recognized me, for she half-way closed her eyes. Placing her hands on Volkmar's epaulettes (those insignia so detested by the Reds that they sometimes nailed them to the flesh of White Russian officers taken captive), she bestowed upon him a second accolade, this time a kiss of defiance. Her partner was gazing down upon her with a sentimental, amorous expression; if love gives that cast to a visage, then women are fools to fall for us, and I am right to mistrust them. With her shoulders showing bare in that blue dress, and her short hair tossed back (she had singed the ends trying to curl them on an iron), Sophie was presenting that bastard the most inviting, and most feigning, pair of lips that ever movie actress offered while keeping a weather eye on the camera. That was too much for me. I took her by the arm and slapped her. The shock, or the surprise, was so great that she staggered backward, stumbled against a chair and fell, so there was a nosebleed to add one more ridiculous touch to the scene.

Volkmar was so dumfounded that he seemed to be counting a measure before tackling me. Rugen intervened and forced me, absurdly enough, into the grandfather chair. Even so we came near to terminating the party with a boxing match: there was a general uproar, above which Volkmar could be heard shouting himself hoarse in demanding apologies; everyone thought we were drunk, and that helped to settle the affair. We were leaving the next day on a dangerous mission; anyhow, who wants to fight with a comrade on Christmas Eve, and for a woman one does not want. They made me shake hands with Volkmar, and the fact is that I was cursing no one but myself for having been such a fool.

As for Sophie, she had vanished amid the swishing of crumpled tulle. In snatching her from her partner I had broken the catch of the small string of pearls she was wearing around her neck, the gift of her grandmother Galitzin on the day of her confirmation. The worthless trinket was lying on the floor. I stooped to pick it up, and mechanically dropped it in my pocket. The occasion never came for giving it back to Sophie; I have often thought of selling it at times when I have been completely flat, but the pearls had discolored and no jeweller would have wanted them. I have the strand still, or rather, I did have it until the small valise where I kept it packed away was stolen from me this year in Spain. There are things like that that you keep without knowing why.

That night my pacing from window to wardrobe was as restless as that of Aunt Prascovia; barefooted, I was hardly apt to wake Conrad, asleep behind his curtain. Some ten different times I fumbled in the dark for my shoes and jacket, deciding to go to Sophie's room again, where this night I was certain to find her alone. Impelled by the absurd craving for precision typical of an immature mind I still asked myself if I loved this girl. To be sure, up to this time there was none of the evidence for passion which even the least carnal-minded among us look for in identifying love, and God knows that in that respect I had harbored a grudge against Sophie for my own reluctance. But the unhappy truth about this girl was that although she seemed utterly promiscuous one could not think of committing oneself to her for less than a lifetime. In a world where everything was heading for a crash I told myself that this woman, at least, would be solid as earth, where one may either build or lie down. It would have been good to begin all over again somewhere with her alone, like two sole survivors of shipwreck. I knew that up to that time I had lived as dangerously and unconventionally as I could; my position would soon become untenable; Conrad would grow old, and I would, too, and war would not always serve as excuse for everything.

Standing there before the wardrobe I debated the wisdom of marriage with Sophie: the decisions against it were not wholly ignoble, but neither were arguments for it wholly disinterested. Affecting complete detachment I asked myself just what I planned to do with this girl; surely I was not prepared to regard Conrad as a brother-in-law. One does not drop a friend of twenty years' standing, though radiantly young, for a shabby intrigue with his sister. Then as if my back-and-forth in the room had brought me to the other extreme of the pendulum I became again for a while that other being within me who readily made light of my personal problems, and who doubtless resembled, feature for feature, all those of my race who before my day had gone in quest of a bride. This fellow, a simpler being than myself, warmed to the thought of a snowy white bosom, as most men do.

Shortly before the hour that the sun was to rise, if the sun did rise on those grey days, I heard the soft, ghostly rustle of feminine garments trembling in the draught of a hall; there was a slight scratching sound like that of a pet animal begging his master to let him in, and the panting of a woman who has run as far as she can toward her one goal. Sophie spoke in a low voice, her mouth close to the oaken door, and the four or five languages that she knew, including French and Russian, helped her to vary those awkward words which in every land are the most abused but still the most pure. Then she concluded,

"Erick, my only true friend, I've come to ask your pardon."

"Sophie, dear, I am getting ready to take off. . . . Come down to the kitchen this morning when we leave. . . . I have something to tell you. . . . Will you forgive me for last night?"

"Erick, I am the one to ask forgiveness. . . ."

Anyone who claims to remember a conversation word for word has always struck me as a mythomaniac, or a liar. I can never recall more than shreds, a text full of holes, like a worm-eaten document. As for my own words, even as I utter them I have ceased to hear them. What the other person says escapes me, too; I retain no more than the memory of lips near enough to kiss. All the rest is only an arbitrary, unnatural reconstruction, and that holds also for the other conversations that I am trying to recollect here. If I do repeat more or less accurately the meagre platitudes exchanged between us that night it is doubtless because they were the last tender things that Sophie ever said to me.

I tried to turn the key noiselessly in the lock in order to join her, but had to give up. We believe that we hesitate, or conversely, that we take a final resolve, but actually it is in such small, temporary decisions that our secret ponderings are betrayed. I was not brave enough to explain the situation to Conrad, and not coward enough, either. Naïvely, he had seen no more in my action of the preceding evening than a protest against liberties taken with his sister by all and sundry; I still do not know whether I should ever have been willing to confess to him that daily, for four months' time, I had lied to him by concealing my involvement with Sophie.

My friend turned in his sleep, moaning involuntarily as his wounded leg rubbed against the sheet; I went back to lie down on my bed, and with my hands clasped under my head I tried to think strictly of the coming day's expedition. If I had taken Sophie that night, I believe that I should have been hungry for the woman whom I had just signalled out, before everyone's eyes, as belonging to me alone. And Sophie, at last made happy, would doubtless have been almost invulnerable to the attacks which were soon to separate us, as it turned out, forever. It is therefore from me that the initiative for any eventual rupture would finally have come: after some weeks of disappointment or delight, my besetting sin would have won me back again; and that indispensable vice, whatever people may think, is much less the love for boys than for solitude. Women cannot live in solitude; they play havoc with it, if doing no more than trying to convert its barrenness into a garden. The being that I am, after all, in what is most inexorably individual about me would have regained the upper hand, and I should have abandoned Sophie whether I wished to or not, much as a ruler abandons a province too far from his center. She would inevitably have turned to Volkmar again, or, if he were not available, then simply to the street.

There are cleaner things than such a succession of

lies and bitter sorrows, reminiscent of some episode between a travelling salesman and a housemaid, and by this time I consider that dire misfortune did not settle matters too badly in the long run. It is none the less true that I have probably lost out on one of the main chances of my life. But there are also some chances which, in spite of ourselves, our instinct rejects.

Towards seven in the morning I went down to the kitchen where Volkmar, ready ahead of time, was waiting for me. Sophie had re-warmed some coffee and assembled some provisions which were no more than leavings from the supper party of the night before; she was impeccable in her care of us, like a soldier's wife. She said goodbye to us in the courtyard, almost at the spot where I had buried Texas on a November night. Not for one moment were we alone together. Although I was prepared to pledge myself to her immediately upon my return, I was nevertheless not sorry to delay my declaration by an interval which could prove to be that of death itself.

All three of us seemed to have forgotten the incidents of the preceding evening: such healing over of wounds, at least such apparent healing, was characteristic of our life so constantly cauterized by war.

Volkmar and I kissed her hand, extended to us each in turn, and she continued to wave to us from afar, making signals that each of us took to be for himself alone. Our men were waiting for us near the barracks huts, crouched around the embers of a fire. It was snowing, and that was to make for harder travel, though protecting us, perhaps, from surprise attacks. The bridges had been blown, but the river was frozen solid. Our object was to reach Munau, where Broussaroff was cut off in a position more exposed than our own; we hoped to cover his retreat if he should have to fall back on our lines.

Telephone communications had been broken for some days between us and Munau, whether because of the storm or enemy action we did not know. Actually, the village had fallen into the hands of the Bolsheviks on Christmas Eve, so the remnant of Broussaroff's hard-pressed troops had been quartered at Gourna. Broussaroff himself was seriously wounded; he died a week later, and in the absence of higher command responsibility for the retreat fell upon me. I attempted a counterattack upon Munau in the hope of regaining some of our men and our captured equipment, but by that move only succeeded in weakening us still more. Broussaroff, in his lucid intervals, persisted in holding on to Gourna, the strategic importance of which he placed far too high; anyhow, I have always thought him a fool, that so-called hero of the 1914 offensive against us in East Prussia.

It was becoming imperative for one of us to go to fetch Rugen at Kratovitsy, and then to proceed to von Wirtz to give him an accurate report on the situation, or rather, two reports, Broussaroff's and my own. If I chose Volkmar for that mission it was because he alone had sufficient address to deal with the Commander-in-Chief, as well as to persuade Rugen to join us; for I have not said that one of Paul's peculiarities was an aversion for Imperial Russian officers that was remarkable even in our ranks, who were almost as unmitigatedly hostile to the White Russian emigrés as to the Bolsheviks themselves. Furthermore, by a curious twist in his conception of professional duty, his devotion to the wounded did not extend beyond the walls of his hospital unit; Broussaroff dying at Gourna interested him less than whatever patient he had operated on last.

Let me be perfectly clear. It is not my desire to be accused of more perfidy than I am capable of conceiving: I was not trying to rid myself of a rival (the word is ludicrous in this case) by sending Volkmar off on a dangerous mission. It was no more hazardous to go back than to stay where we were, nor do I believe that he would have held it against me if I had exposed him to the greater of two risks. He may even have expected such a move on my part; had the circumstances been reversed he would have done the same with me. The only other solution would have been for me to return, myself, to Kratovitsy, leaving Volkmar in command at Gourna, where Broussaroff, already delirious, no longer counted. At the time, Volkmar resented the fact that I assigned him the lesser rôle; as things turned out, he must have been grateful to me later on for having assumed the heavier responsibility. It is not true, either, that I sent him back to Kratovitsy in order to give him a last chance to supplant me in Sophie's affections: those are subtleties that occur to one only in retrospect. I did not distrust the man, as might have been normal between us; contrary to all expectation, he had shown himself to be rather a good sort during those few days that we passed together. In that judgment, as in many other things, I was not sharp enough: his virtues as a comrade-at-arms were not, strictly speaking, hypocritical façade, but a kind of special grace conferred by military status, put on and taken off with his uniform.

I ought to say, too, that Volkmar had a long-standing natural hatred for me, and not merely an animosity inspired by self-interest alone. In his eyes I was an object of scandal, as repugnant, probably, as a spider. He might have thought it his duty to set Sophie on her guard against me; even so, I ought to be grateful to him for not having played that card sooner. I was well aware that I ran some risk in putting him face to face with Sophie again, that is, if she really meant a great deal to me; but it was hardly the moment for considerations of the kind, and in any case my pride would have kept me from dwelling on the matter. As to creating any trouble for me with von Wirtz, I am convinced that he did not do so. Volkmar was an honest man up to a certain point, like everyone else.

Rugen got through to us a few days later, bringing some armoured trucks and a field ambulance. Since our halt at Gourna could not be prolonged I took it upon myself to remove Broussaroff by force; he died on the return journey, as was to be foreseen; he was to prove as great an encumbrance dead as he had been while alive. We were attacked upstream of the village, so I managed to bring no more than a handful of men back to Kratovitsy. My mistakes in the course of that miniature retreat were to stand me in good stead some months after, in operations along the Polish frontier: for each of those men lost at Gourna I saved a dozen lives later on. But never mind that: losers are always wrong, and I deserved all the blame that fell upon me, except for that of failing to obey orders of a dying man whose brain was already affected. Paul's death was the worst blow of all: I had really no other friend. This assertion may seem at variance, I realize, with all that I have said hitherto, but if you think of it for a moment it is fairly easy to reconcile such contradictions.

I passed the first night after my return in the barracks huts, on one of those straw pallets teeming with lice which added typhus to the list of our dangers, but I verily believe that I slept as heavily as the dead. In what concerned Sophie I had not changed my mind; anyhow there had been no time to think about her; but perhaps I was avoiding stepping back immediately into the trap where I now consented to be caught. Everything seemed to me drab, futile, stultifying that night, and more than that, utterly vile.

The next morning, on a foul day of melting snow and west wind, I walked the short distance from the barracks to the main house. To go up to Conrad's office I took the great stairway, now half-blocked with broken packing cases and straw, instead of the service stairs, which I nearly always used. I was neither washed nor shaved, and was therefore completely at a disadvantage in case of a scene, whether for reproaches or for love. It was dark on the staircase, where the shutters were kept securely closed except for one small slit. Between the first and second floor I suddenly found myself running straight into Sophie, who was coming down the steps. She had on her fur-lined jacket and snowboots, and a little wool shawl thrown over her head, much like the silk kerchiefs that women get themselves up in this year at the seaside resorts. She had a bundle in her hand, wrapped up in a kitchen towel knotted at the corners, but then I had often seen her carry similar things on her visits to the hospital or to the gardener's wife. There was nothing new in all that, so the only thing that could have warned me was her expression. But she avoided my eyes.

"So you're starting out, are you, Sophie, in such weather?" I offered this as a mild joke while trying to catch her wrist.

"Yes," she said, "I'm leaving." Her voice told me that this was serious, and that she was really going away.

"Where are you bound?"

"That's of no concern to you," she replied, releasing her wrist with a brusque motion, her throat swelling slightly like a dove's, showing that she had just choked back a sob.

"And may one ask why you are leaving, my dear?"

"I've had all I can stand," she said, and for one instant a convulsive twitching of her lips recalled Aunt Prascovia's tic as she repeated, "I've had enough." With her foolish bundle she looked like a discharged servant girl; shifting it from one arm to the other she made as if to escape, but managed only to come down one step, bringing us nearer together in spite of her effort. Then backing to the wall, so as to leave the greatest space possible between us, she raised her eyes to me for the first time. They were horror-stricken.

"You're a disgusting lot, all of you. . . ." she burst out. I am certain that the words that she next poured forth pell-mell were not hers, nor is it hard to guess their source; it was as if a fountain had suddenly spurted mud. Her face had taken on an expression of peasant grossness: I have seen such explosions of indignation and obscenity in uncouth country girls. It scarcely mattered whether the accusations were justified or not; everything that is said along that line is always false, since the truths of our physical experience escape full utterance in words, and at best can be but half-murmured between lovers.

The situation was becoming clear: this was indeed an adversary confronting me, and the fact that I had always suspected a certain hatred beneath Sophie's abnegation served now to reassure me, at least, upon my discernment. It is conceivable that if I had taken her wholly into my confidence she might have been prevented from going over to the enemy in such fashion, but speculations like that are as idle as trying to prove that Napoleon could have won at Waterloo.

"And it is from Volkmar, I suppose, that you get all this rot?"

"Oh, *him,*" she answered in a tone which left me no doubt as to her feelings for the fellow. At the moment she must have included us together in the same flood of scorn, and with us the rest of mankind.

"What surprises me is that these charming ideas did not come to you long ago," I said, attempting a lighter tone, but trying all the same to draw her into one of those debates in which she would have been lost two months back.

"Oh, they did," she replied absently. "They did, but none of that matters."

Her reply was true enough: nothing is important

for women except themselves, and the choice of anyone else by the men they love appears to them only as a chronic folly, or a passing aberration. I was about to ask her with exasperation what, then, did count for her when suddenly I saw that her face was distorted and her eyelids were quivering with a new onslaught of despair, as if from the painful twinges of neuralgia. Finally she blurted out,

"All the same, I should not have thought that you would have involved Conrad in all that."

She turned her head slightly away; her cheeks, usually so pale, were flaming as if the shame of such an accusation were too great not to fall also upon her. I realized then that Sophie's indifference towards her family, which had long seemed shocking to me, was only a deceiving symptom, an instinctive device for keeping them free of the misery and degradation into which she supposed that she had fallen; her affection for her brother had continued to flow beneath her love for me, welling up like a spring in the salt sea. And more than that, she had invested Conrad with all the privileges and all the virtues which she had renounced, as if that frail boy were the embodiment of her own innocence. The idea that she was defending him against me pricked my guilty conscience at its most vulnerable point. Almost any answer would have been better than the one upon which I now stumbled in my embarrassment and anger, and in my haste to strike back. Deep down within every one of us lurks an insolent, dull-witted cad: it was he who retorted,

"Street walkers should hardly take over the policing of public morals, my friend."

She looked at me with astonishment, as if, after all, she had not expected that; too late I perceived that denial of what she had charged would have filled her with joy, or, quite the reverse, that admission of the truth on my part would doubtless have drawn from her nothing more than a flood of tears. Bending toward me, her brows contracted, she sought some reply for that single short sentence which was making for greater division between us than any vice, avowed or concealed, but finding nothing in her mouth more useful than saliva she simply spat in my face. I stood there, in a daze, watching her descend the stairs. Her step was heavy but swift. On reaching the bottom she happened to catch her jacket on a nail of a packing case; she jerked it free but tore a whole piece of the otter skin lining. A minute later I heard the door of the vestibule close.

I dried my face with my sleeve before going on up to Conrad. The crackling sound of the telegraph, like a sewing machine or machine gun, came from the other side of the half-opened study door. Conrad was working with his back to the window, his elbows planted on the massive, carved oak table. That was the room where his grandfather before him, with his mania for hunting trophies, had assembled a grotesque collection of antlered heads and tusks. A crazy, weird array of small stuffed animals was lined up along the shelves; I shall always remember a certain squirrel decked out in a vest and a Tyrolese hat over his moth-eaten fur. There in that odor of camphor and naphtalene I passed some of the most critical moments of my life.

On seeing me enter, Conrad barely raised his head; his face was pale and haggard from overwork and anxiety. I noticed that the lock of hair that persisted in falling on his forehead was less abundant and less glossy than before; he would have been slightly bald in ten years' time. Conrad was enough of a Russian, after all, to be one of Broussaroff's fanatic admirers; he thought me in the wrong, perhaps all the more so that he had worn himself out with worry on my behalf. At my very first words he interrupted me:

"Volkmar didn't consider Broussaroff fatally wounded."

"Volkmar is no doctor," I rejoined, and the shock of that name released all my resentment against the personage, although I had not been aware of it ten minutes before. "Paul declared at once that Broussaroff had less than forty-eight hours to live. . . ."

"And since Paul is no longer alive there is only your word for it."

"Why not say straight out that you wished I hadn't come back?"

"Oh, you're disgusting, all of you!" he exclaimed, clapping his slender hands to his head in a movement of despair; I was struck by the identity of his outcry with that of the fugitive girl. Brother and sister had the same absolute integrity, and were equally intolerant and stubborn.

My friend never forgave me the loss of that imprudent, ill-informed old general, but publicly he always supported, to the end of his life, the very conduct which privately he judged inexcusable. Standing at the window I listened without interrupting as he talked; in fact, I hardly heard him. My attention was wholly absorbed by a lone figure outlined against a landscape of mud and snow, under a grey sky, and my one fear was that Conrad would get up, limping his way over to me, to cast a glance outside in his turn. The window looked down on the courtyard and the road; beyond the old bakehouse a turning led to the village of Marba, on the opposite bank of the pond. Sophie walked with difficulty, her heavy boots sinking into the mud, leaving enormous imprints behind her; she was bending forward, blinded no doubt by the wind and snow, and her bundle made her look from afar like a pedlar. I held my breath until her beshawled head had disappeared behind the sagging wall that bordered the road. Conrad was still speaking: the blame that he heaped upon me I accepted as my due in exchange for more just reproaches which he would have had the right to make had he realized that I was letting Sophie go off alone, in a direction unknown, and probably never to come back.

I am sure that at that moment she had only courage enough to walk straight on without turning to look behind; Conrad and I could easily have overtaken her and brought her home by force. But that was just what I was not willing to do; first, out of resentment, and then because after what had happened between her and me I could not endure seeing that same tense situation reestablish itself and go on, unchanged, as before; and partly out of curiosity, too, were it only to give events the chance to develop by themselves. One thing at least was clear: she was not going to throw herself into Volkmar's arms. And contrary to the thought that had momentarily crossed my mind, that abandoned towpath did not lead to the Red outposts.

I knew Sophie too well not to recognize the fact that, once gone, she would never again consent to be seen alive at Kratovitsy, but in spite of everything I was certain that one day or other we should meet somewhere face to face. Even if I had known what the circumstances of that meeting would be, I doubt if I should have done anything to prevent her departure. Sophie was not a child, and I respect my fellow beings enough, in my way, not to interfere with their own decisions.

Strange as it may seem, nearly thirty hours passed before her disappearance was noticed at all. As was to be expected, it was Chopin who gave the alarm.

He had met Sophie the day before, about noon, at the point where the road to Marba leaves the pond's bank and enters the little pine grove. She had asked him for a cigarette; his supply was running out, but he had shared with her the last of his packet. They had sat together on the old bench which was still in place there, a rickety reminder of the days when the whole pond was comprised within the bounds of the park; she had asked news of Chopin's wife, who had just had a child in a hospital clinic in Warsaw. When she left him Sophie had cautioned him to keep quiet about their encounter:

"Above all, not a word about me. The point is, old boy, it's Erick who sends me."

Chopin was used to seeing her carry dangerous messages for me; he disapproved of me for it, but only silently so. The next day, however, he asked me if I had assigned the girl some mission in the direction of Marba. I had to limit myself to a shrug of negative reply; Conrad, upset, insisted upon an answer, and there was nothing for it but to lie and to declare that I had not seen Sophie again since my return. It would have been wiser to admit that I had passed her on the stairway, but when one lies it is almost always for oneself, trying to bury some memory.

On the following day several Russian refugees newly arrived at Kratovitsy said something about a young peasant girl in a fur-lined jacket whom they had met along the way, resting beside a hut where they had stopped to take shelter during a snowflurry. They had exchanged greetings with her and a few jokes, hampered somewhat by their ignorance of the local dialect, and she had offered them some of her bread. One of them had asked her some questions in German after that, but she had replied by shaking her head "No," as if she understood only the speech of the region. Chopin urged Conrad to organize search parties in the area, but these produced no clues. All the farms in the direction of Marba had been abandoned, and the solitary tracks to be found on the snow could have belonged just as well to a soldier, or a tramp. The next day the weather was such as to discourage even Chopin from going on with his search, and a new attack from the Reds forced us to think of other things than Sophie's departure.

Conrad had not made me his sister's keeper, and

it was not I, after all, who had sent her on her way, at least, not voluntarily so. Nevertheless, during those long nights the picture of the young girl splashing along in the mud and the cold haunted my sleepless hours as relentlessly as if she had been a ghost. And the truth is that after she died Sophie never came back to pursue me as she did at the time of her disappearance.

By dint of much reflection upon the circumstances of her departure I came upon a trail which I kept to myself. I had long suspected that the recapture of Kratovitsy from the Bolsheviks had not completely broken all relations between Sophie and the former bookstore clerk, Gregory Loew. Now the road to Marba led also to Lilienkron, where Loew's mother practised the lucrative, two-fold profession of dress-maker and midwife. Her husband, Jacob Loew, had engaged in the almost equally official and still more lucrative practice of usury (for a long time without his son's knowing it, I really believe, and thereafter to the latter's utter disgust). In the course of repris-als taken by troops on our side, the elder Loew had been shot by some debtor on the threshold of his second-hand shop, and was now elevated to the rank of martyr in the small Jewish community in the town of Lilienkron. As for the wife, although she was suspect from every point of view, since her son held a command in the Bolshevik army, she had succeeded up to this time in keeping her standing in the community; such adroitness, or else such subservience, hardly predisposed me in her favor.

After all, the Loew household with its sitting room done up in scarlet rep and its porcelain gas lamp had been the only thing that Sophie had ever sought out for herself beyond Kratovitsy, and from the moment that she left us she could hardly have turned to anyone but them. I knew, too, that she had consulted Mother Loew at the time that she thought herself threatened with disease or with pregnancy after that rape, her first disaster. For a girl like her, to have confided once already in this Jewish matron was reason to trust to her again, and forever. Besides, as I was to be sufficiently discerning to see at a glance, in spite of my most cherished prejudices, the face of that old creature, fairly drowned in her own fat, was marked with obvious kindness. We had forced all the roughness of military life upon Sophie, but the free-masonry of womankind still existed between those two.

On the pretext of levying supplies I set out for Lilienkron, taking with me a few men in an old armored truck. The creaking vehicle came to a stop before a somewhat citified house on the edge of town: Mother Loew was hanging out her washing in the February sun, and was making good use of the drying space in the next garden, left abandoned by neighbors who had long since been evacuated. I recognized Sophie's short, torn coat: the old woman wore it over her black dress and white linen apron, and it looked absurdly tight around her thick waist. Our search revealed only the usual number of enamel basins and antiseptics, sewing machines and tattered copies of fashion books from Berlin some two years old. While my men went through the wardrobes filled with old clothes (left in pawn at the midwife's by patients short of cash), Mother Loew made me sit down on the red upholstered sofa in the dining room. Though refusing to explain to me how she had come by Sophie's jacket, she insisted that I take at least a glass of tea: revolting obsequiousness blended here with truly Biblical hospitality.

Such extreme courtesy finally seemed to me suspect: I reached the kitchen just in time to keep some ten messages, from her dear Gregory, from being consumed in the flame that burned under the samovar. Mother Loew had preserved those compromising letters out of a kind of maternal superstition, but the latest of them was dated at least fifteen days before, and consequently could tell me nothing of what I sought. Even if those half-charred scraps of paper contained only futile testimony to filial affection the old Jewess was none the less heading for execution; and they still could signify a code. The evidence was more than sufficient to justify such a verdict, even in the eyes of the principal concerned, so when we sat down on the sofa again she resigned herself to compromise between silence and open avowal. She confessed that Sophie had come there exhausted on a Thursday evening and had stayed to rest; she had left in the middle of the night. As to the purpose of her visit I gathered not the slightest information at first.

"She wanted to see me, that's all," said the old Jewess in an enigmatic tone; her eyes, still fine in spite of their puffy lids, blinked nervously.

"Was she pregnant?" That was not mere wanton brutality on my part: a man goes searching far afield for suppositions in the absence of certitude.

Had one of Sophie's last adventures had any consequences the girl would have fled from me, assuredly, exactly as she had done, and the quarrel on the stairway would have served to screen the true reason for her departure.

"Listen, Mr. Officer. Someone like the young Countess, she's not the same as one of these peasant girls."

She ended by admitting that Sophie had come to Lilienkron with the intention of borrowing some of Gregory's clothes in order to dress as a man: "She tried them on right here where you are, Mister Officer. I couldn't very well refuse her that. But the clothes didn't fit; she was too tall."

I recalled, true enough, that Sophie at the age of sixteen was already a head taller than the frail little bookstore clerk. It was comical to think of her trying to get into Gregory's jacket and trousers. Mother Loew had offered her some peasant women's dresses, but Sophie had held to her first idea, and they had finally hunted out some men's garments that would do. A guide, too, had been provided for her.

"Who is the guide?"

"He has not come back yet," was all the old Jewess would say, and her chaps began to tremble.

"And because he is not back yet you have no letter from your son this week. Where are they?"

"If I knew, Sir, I don't think I should tell you," she rejoined, with a certain dignity. "But even supposing that I knew it a few days ago, you surely realize that my information would be out of date by this time."

Her answer was common sense itself; the fat old woman was not lacking in inner courage in spite of betraying all the signs of physical terror. Her hands folded in her lap were trembling convulsively, but bayonets would have been of as little avail against her as against the mother of the Maccabees. I had already resolved to spare her life. After all, she had done no more than enter into the bewildering game that Sophie and I were playing against each other. My mercy hardly helped, for some soldiers killed the old Jewess a few weeks later; but so far as I was concerned I could as well have crushed a caterpillar as harm that poor creature. Had I had Gregory or Volkmar up before me I should have been less indulgent.

"And the young lady doubtless had confided her project to you some time ago?"

"No. There was some question of it last autumn,"

she added, with that timid side glance which seeks to ascertain just how much the questioner knows already. "She had not spoken about it to me again since then."

"Very well," I concluded, rising and at the same time thrusting the packet of Gregory's charred letters into one of my pockets. I was only too glad to leave the room; Sophie's jacket, thrown over a corner of the sofa, depressed me; it was like a dog without his mistress. To my dying day I shall be persuaded that the old woman had exacted it in payment for her help.

"You know to what risks you have exposed yourself in helping someone procure conduct to the enemy lines?"

"My son told me to put myself at the disposal of the young Countess," replied the midwife, who seemed little concerned with the new terminology of the times. "If she has managed to join him," she added, as if in spite of herself, and her voice could not restrain a cackle of pride, "I think that my Gregory and she will have married. That makes things easier, too."

In the truck on the way back to Kratovitsy I had to laugh at my ill-placed solicitude: young Mrs.

Loew indeed! To be sure, all probabilities were that Sophie's body was lying at that very moment in a ditch, or behind a thicket, her knees doubled up under her and her hair spattered with earth, like an injured partridge or pheasant brought down by some poacher. Of all the possible solutions I should naturally have preferred that one.

I concealed from Conrad nothing of what I had learned at Lilienkron. Perhaps I needed to share the bitterness of the blow with someone. Clearly Sophie had acted on the kind of impulse that drives girls when seduced, or women abandoned, to enter a convent or a brothel, even if they do not incline toward such dramatic extremes. The factor of Loew, however, was decidedly in the way of my effort to take a romantic view of her departure. Sophie was hardly to blame for such an anti-climax; I already knew enough of the world by that time to see that the minor characters in our lives (Loew was simply that for her) are not of our own choosing. The one obstacle to development of Sophie's revolutionary leanings had been me, but from the moment she wrenched love for me from her heart she inevitably gave herself over completely to a course marked out by her early readings and the excitement of her friendship with young Gregory; she was further impelled on her way by the distaste which unsentimental souls feel for the environment in which they have grown up.

But Conrad had the failing, a nervous symptom, I suppose, of never being able to accept facts for what they are, without stretching them for dubious meanings and hypotheses. I was afflicted with the same vice, but my suppositions remained problematical and did not pass over into myth or some form of cheap fiction. The more Conrad reflected on Sophie's silent departure, with no letter or parting kiss, the more he conjectured that her motives for disappearing were suspect, and therefore better left obscure. That long winter at Kratovitsy had made complete strangers of the brother and sister, such as only two members of the same family can manage to become. After my return from Lilienkron Sophie ceased to be more for Conrad than a spy whose former presence among us accounted for all our reverses, and even for my recent disaster at Gourna.

I was as sure of Sophie's integrity as of her courage, and such idiotic accusations very nearly made a breach in our friendship: I have always thought it low to believe so readily in others' disgrace. My esteem for Conrad suffered accordingly, until I began to realize that making Sophie into a Mata-Hari of the screen or of conventional spy stories was perhaps my friend's naïve way of honoring his sister, and of attributing to her face and great, troubled eyes that striking beauty which she already possessed, but which, like all brothers, he had been too blind to appreciate before. Worse still, the shock and indignation of Chopin were so strong that he accepted Conrad's romanticized explanations without a word of dissent. Chopin had adored Sophie; his disillusionment was now too great for him to do anything but revile the idol turned traitor.

Of the three of us I was certainly least pure in heart, but I was the only one, nevertheless, who trusted Sophie and who was trying already to pronounce upon her the verdict of acquittal that she might rightfully have rendered to herself, all things considered, at the moment of her death. The fact is that pure hearts nurse not a few prejudices from which the cynic is free, just as he is free of scruples. It is true, too, that I was the only one to gain more than he lost in her disappearance, and that, as so often happens in my life, I could not help greeting that disaster like an accomplice. They say that fate excels in tightening the cord round the victim's neck, but to my knowledge her special skill is to break all ties. In the long run, and whether we wish it or not, destiny extracts us from difficulties by removing them, and everything else, from us.

From that time on, Sophie was as dead and buried for us as if I had brought her body back from Lilienkron riddled by bullets. The change made by her departure was out of all proportion to the place which she had seemingly occupied in our midst: calm now reigned in this house without women (for Aunt Prascovia was but a phantom), a peace like that of a monastery, or a tomb. Our ever diminishing group was returning to the great traditions of austerity and manly courage; Kratovitsy was becoming again what it had been in times supposedly gone by, an outpost of the Teutonic Order, a frontier fortress of the Livonian Brothers of the Sword. When, in spite of everything that occurred there, I identify Kratovitsy with a certain ideal of happiness, I think of that period, too, quite as much as the days of my childhood.

Europe was betraying us: Lloyd George's government favored the Soviets; von Wirtz was going back to Germany, definitely abandoning the Russo-Baltic embroilments; negotiations at Dorpat had long since removed all legal basis, and almost all meaning, from our small center of obstinate but futile resistance. On the southern shore of the Russian continent Wrangel, succeeding Denikin, was signing the lamentable declaration of Sebastopol, somewhat as a man might sign his own death sentence. And the victorious offensive on the Polish front had not yet come to arouse hopes in that quarter, hopes soon to be dashed by the armistice of September, and the eventual crushing of the Crimea.

But this summary that I am dishing up to you is made in retrospect, like History itself; none of these events alter the fact that during those few weeks I lived as free from worry as if I were to die the next day, or else live on forever. Danger brings out what is best in the human soul, but the worst, also. Since the bad usually predominates, the atmosphere of war is, on the whole, thoroughly debasing; still, that is no reason to undervalue the rare moments of grandeur that it affords. If I remember the air of Kratovitsy as bracing to the virtues of loyalty and courage it is doubtless because I had there the privilege of living with beings who were instinctively pure.

Natures like Conrad's are frail, so they feel at their best when clad in armor. But turned loose in the world of society or of business, lionized by women or a prey to easy success, they are subject to certain insidious dissolution, like the loathsome decay of iris; those sombre flowers, though nobly shaped like a lance, die miserably in their own sticky secretion, in marked contrast to the slow, heroic drying of the rose. I have known almost all the baser feelings in my life, each of them at least once, so I cannot say that I am impervious to fear, but Conrad did not know even the meaning of the word. There are such beings, often the most fragile of all, who live at ease with death, as if in their native element. One often hears of this special gift, almost an investiture, in consumptive patients destined to die young; but I have sometimes seen youths who were headed for violent death manifesting that same lightness of heart which is both their essential virtue and their privilege as young gods.

Towards the third of May, on a day of soft, hazy spring sunlight, we sorrowfully abandoned Kratovitsy, now no longer defendable. For the last time we crossed its melancholy park, transformed since then into sports fields for Soviet workers, and its ruined forests where up to the first years of the war herds of auroch roamed, the last of their kind surviving from prehistoric times. Aunt Prascovia had refused to leave, so we had entrusted her to the care of the old housemaid. Later on I learned that she had outlived all our woes.

The road had been cut to the north of us, but my hope was to effect a junction with the anti-Bolshevik forces in the southwest section of the country; and I did succeed, as a matter of fact, in getting through to the Polish army in five weeks' time, when it was still at the height of its first offensive. To achieve so desperate a break-through I was counting for help upon the revolt of the peasants in the district, worn down by famine; nor was I mistaken in them; but starving as they were, they were in no condition to replenish our supplies, so hunger and typhus together took their toll of our men before we finally reached Vitna.

I have already said, some time ago, that the Kratovitsy of our youth, at the beginning of the war, meant Conrad for me, and not my own boyhood; it may be, too, that that entire retreat still means Conrad for me, and not war, or a marginal adventure in a lost cause. He it was who made unforgettable that mixture of destitution and grandeur in everything around us: the forced marches along roadways lined with willows, their branches trailing in the flooded fields; volleys of firing followed by sudden stillness; hunger pangs in griping bellies while stars trembled overhead in those pale nights, a trembling such as I have never seen since. When I think of those last days of my friend's life I evoke, almost automatically, a picture of Rembrandt's not widely known, in the Frick Gallery of New York. I discovered it by chance on a morning of snow-storm when I had nothing else to do, and the impression it made upon me was that of a ghost who had acquired an accession number and a place in the catalogue: that youth, mounted on a pale horse, half turning in his saddle as he rides swiftly on, his face both sensitive and fierce, a desolate landscape where the nervous animal seems to sense disaster ahead, and Death and the Devil infinitely more in attendance there than in Durer's engraving (for to feel them near one has no need of their symbol . . .).

In Manchuria I hardly distinguished myself, and in the Spanish war, I am happy to say, I kept to a minor rôle, but in the course of that retreat from Kratovitsy my abilities as a commander were given full play; for a handful of men, at that, but the only group to whom I ever felt bound by strong human ties. Compared to those Slavs, who were only too ready to founder in fatal despair, I represented the soul of logic and order, and the precision of an ordnance map. In the village of Novogrodno we were attacked by a detachment of Cossack cavalry. Conrad, Chopin, and I with some fifty men fell back to the cemetery where we were separated from the main body of our troops, quartered in the hamlet, by a broad hollow, something like the palm of a hand. Towards evening the last of the enemy horse disappeared, crossing the rye fields, but Conrad, shot in the belly, lay dying.

My fear was that his courage might suddenly fail

him for the bad half hour to come (longer than his whole life had been), that same courage which often rises unexpectedly in those who have trembled till then. But when it was finally possible for me to turn my attention to him he had already passed that invisible line of demarcation beyond which one no longer fears to die. Chopin had stuffed the wound with one of those packets of bandage which we were saving with such care; for less grave wounds we used dried moss. Night began to fall: Conrad kept calling for light feebly, insistently, childishly, as if darkness were the worst of death. I lighted one of those iron lanterns that they hang on the tombstones in that region. Such a lamp, visible from afar in the clear night air, could have attracted firing upon us, but that was the least of my concerns, as you may well imagine.

He suffered so much that I thought more than once of putting him out of his agony; sheer cowardice held me back. In those few hours I saw him age, and almost saw him go back through the centuries: first he was like a wounded officer of the time of Charles the Twelfth, then like a medieval knight lying upon a tomb, and finally like any dying man without trace of caste or period, a young peasant or a boatman of those northern provinces from which his family had originally come. He died at dawn, wholly unrecognizable and nearly unconscious, half-choked with rum by Chopin and me in turn: we spelled each other in holding the glass, full to the brim, at the level of his lips, and in keeping the avid swarms of mosquitoes away from his face.

Day was breaking; we had to go, but I clung fiercely to the notion of some kind of burial service; I could not have him merely covered over like a dog in a corner of that broken-down cemetery. Leaving Chopin with him I crossed through the lines of tombs, stumbling in the uncertain daylight upon other wounded men, to get to the rectory at the far side of the graveyard. The priest had passed the night in the cellar, fearing renewal of the firing at any moment; when I knocked at his door he was speechless with fright, and I believe that I actually got him out with the butt of my rifle. Slightly reassured by the nature of my request he consented to follow me, book in hand; but as soon as he was reinstated in his function, which was that of prayer, the unmistakable grace of his office obtained, and the brief absolution of the body was given with as much solemnity as in a cathedral choir.

I had the curious feeling of having brought Conrad safely into port: slain in warfare and blessed by a priest, he was completing a destiny of the type which his ancestors would have approved; furthermore, he was spared what the future would bring. My personal regrets have nothing to do with that view, to which I have newly subscribed each day of these past twenty years; the years to come will probably not make me change my opinion that for him such a death was a happy chance.

After that, except for what concerns purely strategic detail, there is a blank in my memory. There are periods in each person's life, I suppose, when a man really exists, and others when he is only an agglomeration of responsibilities, strain, and (for feebler heads) vanity. At night, unable to sleep as I lay on some sacks in a barn, I would read an odd volume brought with me from a set at Kratovitsy, Cardinal de Retz's *Memoirs;* if utter lack of hope and illusion is what characterizes the dead, then that bed of mine was not essentially different from the one in which Conrad's body was beginning to dissolve. But I am well aware that between the dead and the living there will always be some mysterious interval; we do not know its nature, and even the best informed among us are no better instructed about death than a spinster is about love. If by dying we attain to something like promotion in rank, then I grant that Conrad had earned such superior rating.

As for Sophie, she had gone completely out of my mind. Just as a woman taken leave of in the street grows less distinct in moving farther away, and eventually becomes a passer-by like the rest, the feelings which Sophie had inspired in me were receding in the distance into what is most commonplace in love; no more was left to me from those emotions than one of those faded recollections which brings a shrug when one finds it deep in one's memory, like a snapshot blurred, or taken against the light, in the course of some stroll, now forgotten. But since that time the picture has been further developed, by means of a bath in acid.

I was worn out; a little later on, in fact, I practically slept for a month, after my return to Germany. All the end of this story took place in an atmosphere which is less that of dream or nightmare than of heavy sleep. I even slept standing up, like a tired horse. I am not trying to plead irresponsibility; what wrong I could do to Sophie had long been done, and the most deliberate intention could not have added much more. It is certain that in all that last act to come I had only a secondary part, and somnambulistic at that. You may tell me that in romantic melodrama there were mute rôles, too, some of them highly conspicuous, like that of the executioner. But I have the distinct impression that after a certain moment it was Sophie who took over the command of her own destiny; and I know that I am not mistaken, since I have sometimes fallen so low as to resent it. Since so little was left to her, we may as well credit her with the initiative for her death.

Fate closed its circle around the two of us in the small village of Kovo, at the junction of two streams with unpronounceable names; it happened only a few days before the arrival of Polish troops. The river had overflowed its bed at the end of the spring's high water, transforming the district into a sodden, muddy island where at least we were more or less protected from any attack from the North. Nearly all enemy troops in that area had been diverted from other fronts to the West, to meet the Polish offensive. Compared to this desolate countryside, the surroundings of Kratovitsy had been prosperous, indeed. We took the village almost without difficulty; three quarters of its inhabitants had died of famine, or as victims of the recent executions; we also occupied the buildings of the small railway station, standing unused since the close of the Great War; old wooden cars were rotting there on the rusty rails. The shattered remnants of a Bolshevik regiment returning from the Polish front had quartered themselves in the former spinning mill, established at Kovo before that war by a Swiss industrialist. Although they were nearly out of food and munitions, they were still well enough supplied that their reserves were to help us, eventually, to hold on until the arrival of the Polish division who saved us.

The Warner mill stood in the middle of flooded land: I can still see its line of low sheds against the stormy sky; they were already lapped by the river's dark waters disastrously swollen from the recent rains. Several of our men were drowned in that mud where one sank to the waist, like duck hunters in a swamp. The Reds' tenacious resistance gave way only after further high water swept off a section of the buildings, undermined by five years of exposure and neglect. Our men fought as desperately to take these few sheds as if the assault helped to settle an old score with the enemy.

One of the first corpses that I came upon as I entered the Warner mill was Gregory Loew's. He still had an aspect, even in death, of shy student and obsequious clerk, not that that kept him from having dignity, too, as nearly all the dead do. So I was destined to meet sooner or later my only two personal enemies, each in positions infinitely more stable than my own, thus practically eliminating any notion of vengeance. For I saw Volkmar again while I was in South America, in diplomatic service for his country in Caracas, with a brilliant career ahead of him; and as if to make any attempt at vengeance on my part more impossible still, he had simply forgotten the whole affair. Gregory Loew was even farther beyond my reach. I had his body searched, but found not a single paper in his pockets which could tell me of Sophie's fate. On the other hand, he did have a copy of Rilke's *Book of Hours;* Conrad had loved it, too. This Gregory was probably the only man in the land at the time with whom I might have had half an hour's decent conversation. It must be admitted that the Jewish passion for rising above the paternal pawnshop had produced certain excellent psychological results in young Loew, his devotion to a cause, his love for lyric poetry, his friendship for an ardent young girl, and finally, the somewhat too common privilege of dying a gallant death.

A handful of soldiers were still holding out in the hayloft of a barn. The long gallery was raised on piles which swayed under pressure of the water and finally collapsed, bringing down a few men clutching to an enormous beam. Forced to choose between drowning and execution, the survivors had to surrender, without illusion as to what their fate would be. No one took prisoners any more on either side; how could we drag them along with us in such devastation? One by one, six or seven exhausted men lurched their way down the steep ladder-stairs leading from the hayloft to the shed. Bales of moldy flax encumbered the place, for this shed had once served as the storehouse. The first to descend, a young blond giant wounded in the hip, reeled, missed a step, and fell to the ground, where someone finished him off. Suddenly I recognized at the very top of the stairs a head of tangled blond hair, extraordinarily fair and identical with the one which I had watched disappearing beneath the earth three weeks before. Michael, the old gardener who had come with me from Kratovitsy in the vague guise of orderly, looked up, half-stupefied as he was by all that had happened, and exclaimed, dully,

"The young mistress. . . ."

It was indeed Sophie, and she nodded to me from afar with the casual indifference of a woman who recognizes someone but has no wish to be accosted. Shod and clad like the others, she would have been taken for a very young soldier. Swiftly, easily she strode past the small group gathered hesitantly together in the dust and semi-darkness to get to the tall, fair youth stretched out at the base of the ladder. She looked down upon him with the same expression, both hard and tender, with which she had gazed on the dog Texas that night in November; then she knelt to close his eyes. When she rose again her face had resumed its blank composure, calm, even, and unchanging, like tilled fields under an autumn sky. The captives were ordered to help transport the reserves of munitions and food to the station house of Kovo. Sophie was last in line, not carrying anything, and assuming the indifferent air of a boy who has just managed to get exempted from a chore; she was whistling *Tipperary.*

Chopin and I followed in their footsteps at some distance, and our two faces must have revealed our consternation, like relatives at a funeral. We were silent; each of us at that moment sought to save the girl, and each suspected the other of opposing his project. For Chopin, at least, that fit of leniency was soon over; within a few hours he had resolved upon extreme rigor as firmly as Conrad would have done in his place. To gain time I turned to the task of examining the prisoners. We shut them into a cattle car left standing on the tracks, and they were brought to me one by one in the station master's office. The first to be questioned, a peasant of Little Russia, grasped not a word of what, merely for form's sake, I was asking him, so deadened he was by fatigue, long-suffering resignation, or utter indifference to all. He was full thirty years my senior; I have never felt so young and inadequate as when confronting that simple farmer old enough to have been my father. Sickened by the whole proceeding, I sent him away. Sophie came next, ushered in by two soldiers who might as well have been announcing her in the course of a society ball. For the span of a second I could read in her face that one special fear which is no more than dread of losing one's courage. She came to the deal table at which I was seated and spoke very fast:

"Don't expect any information from me, Erick. I shall say nothing, and I know nothing."

"It is not for information that I have had you come," and I motioned her to take a chair. She hesitated, then sat down.

"For what, then?"

"For some explanations on your part. Did you know that Gregory Loew is dead?"

She nodded an affirmative, gravely but without sorrow. She had looked exactly like that at Kratovitsy when told of the death of comrades of ours who meant much to her, but only as friends.

"I saw his mother at Lilienkron last month. She assured me that you and Gregory had married."

"Who? Me? What an idea!" she answered in French, and the sound of those few words was enough to take me back to the Kratovitsy of other days.

"Nevertheless, you were lovers, weren't you?"

"What an idea!" she repeated. "It's the same as for

Volkmar: you thought that we were engaged. You know very well that I used to tell you everything," she said calmly, with her usual childlike simplicity. But then she added somewhat sententiously:

"Gregory was a very fine person."

"I begin to think so myself," I agreed. "But how about this wounded fellow whom you were tending just now?"

"Yes," and she seemed to muse. "We have stayed closer friends than I thought, all the same, Erick, since you have guessed about him." She clasped her hands pensively and the vague look came into her eyes again, as if she were gazing beyond the person to whom she was speaking, a trait of the near-sighted, but also of those absorbed in a single thought, or a memory.

"He was very kind. I don't know what I should have done without him," she continued, but in the tone of a lesson literally learned by heart.

"Have things been difficult for you, over there?"

"No, I was happy."

I recalled that I had been happy, too, during that sinister spring. The serenity emanating from her was the kind that comes from having known satisfaction in its most basic, most substantial form. Such tranquillity can never be completely shaken. Had she found it with this man, or did it grow out of the constant adjustment to danger and the imminence of death? However that may be, she was no longer in love with me at the moment: she had no further concern for effects produced upon me.

"And now?" I asked, indicating to her meanwhile a box of cigarettes open upon the table, but she refused them.

"Now?" she echoed. Her tone was surprised.

"You have some relatives in Poland, haven't you?"

"Oh, you think of taking me back to Poland. Is that Conrad's notion, too?"

"Conrad is dead." I said it as simply as I could.

"I am sorry, Erick," she answered gently, as if the loss concerned me alone.

I came back to the matter in hand. "Are you actually so determined to die?"

Sincere replies are never clear-cut, or swift. She thought for a moment, half frowning, and that gave her brow the wrinkles that she would probably have had in twenty years' time. I sat there watching that mysterious weighing of imponderables which a Lazarus doubtless attempted too late, after his resurrection: fear of death was being balanced against the fatigue of living, courage against despair; the desire to consume a few more meals, sleep a few more nights, and see the sun rise again was thrown into one scale, and into the other the feeling of having lived fully enough. Perhaps added to that were two or three dozen memories, good and bad, the kind which, according to our natures, help to deter us from, or precipitate us into, death. Finally she spoke, and her response was as much to the point as possible, I suppose:

"What are you going to do with the others?"

I did not answer, and my silence told all. She rose, with the air of someone who has failed to conclude the deal in hand, but who personally has little at stake.

"As far as you are concerned," said I, rising in my turn, "You know that I will do my utmost. I can promise nothing more."

"I'm not asking that much," was her answer, and half turning about she traced with her finger something on the steamy window pane which she immediately erased.

"You don't wish to be in my debt?"

"It's not even that," and she let the point drop, as if less and less interested in the conversation.

I had moved a few steps towards her, fascinated, in spite of everything that had passed between us, by this creature now clothed for me with the two-fold prestige of a soldier and of a woman about to die. If I could have given way to my inclination I suppose that I should have stammered some incoherent words of affection, which she most certainly would have been pleased to reject with scorn. But how find words not abused for so long a time as to have wholly lost their meaning? I admit, though, that this difficulty existed only because something had seriously deteriorated within us both: our sombre experience had left us with distrust for words, and with distrust for more than words alone. A genuine love could still have saved us, her from the immediate present and me from the future. But such a love had crossed Sophie's path only in the guise of a young Russian peasant who lay beaten to death in a barn.

Awkwardly, as if to assure myself that her heart was still beating, I placed my hands on her breast. I could find nothing more to say than to repeat once again,

"I will do my best."

"Don't try any more, Erick," she said, releasing herself without my knowing whether she referred to my gesture as a lover, or to my promise. "It doesn't suit you." And returning to the table she rang a small bell which she had spied there, forgotten on the station master's desk. A soldier came to lead her away. Not until she was gone did I notice that she had filched my cigarettes.

Probably no one slept that night, Chopin least of all. We two were supposed to share the station-master's scantly padded couch: all night long I watched Chopin pacing the room, matched by his shadow along the wall, a stout man collapsed with woe. Two or three times he paused before me, placing a hand on my arm, meditatively shaking his head; then he would resume his heavy tread, back and forth, resigned. He knew as I did that if we had proposed to our comrades to spare this girl, and her only, although she was renegade in the eyes of all, we should have been dishonored and nothing gained. I turned towards the wall, not to see him; otherwise it would have been hard not to curse him out. Still, he was the one I pitied most. As for Sophie, I could not think of her without a kind of sickening fury in the pit of my stomach that made me say "all the better" for her death. But then reaction set in, and I seemed to be beating my head against the inevitable, like a prisoner at the wall of his cell.

What was horrible to me was not so much Sophie's death as her obstinate will to die. I felt that a better man than I would have found some admirable expedient, but then I have never had any illusion as to my inadequacy in impassioned appeal. With Conrad's sister gone my youth, at least, would be over for good and the last bridge cut between that country and me. Finally I fell to recalling the other deaths I had witnessed, as if Sophie's execution could have been justified by them! Then, reflecting upon the low value placed on the human commodity, I told myself I was making much ado over the corpse of a woman which would have moved me hardly at all had I discovered it already cold in the corridor of Warner's factory.

When morning came at last, Chopin preceded me to the levelled strip of ground between the station and the communal barn. The prisoners, huddled together on a siding, looked even more exhausted, if possible, than the day before; those of our men who had been detailed to guard them seemed almost as far gone themselves, having no strength now for such extra duty; the effort which I had felt obliged to make to save Sophie, had had no other result than to give everyone just one bad night more. She was sitting on a pile of wood, knees apart and hands hanging free between them, like one deep in thought; with the heels of her heavy shoes she had hollowed small furrows, mechanically, into the soil. She was smoking in rapid succession the cigarettes so deftly acquired, but that was her only sign of anguish; the fresh morning air had brought a healthy color to her cheeks. Her eyes were fixed, and seemed not to notice my presence. Had it been the reverse I doubtless would have lost what control I still had. She looked too much like her brother, after all, for me to avoid the feeling of seeing him die twice.

It was Michael who always took over the rôle of executioner on these occasions, as though in this way he were only continuing his function as butcher at Kratovitsy, a duty he performed when by chance there was any cattle to slaughter for our food. Chopin had given the order that Sophie was to be executed last of all; to this day I still do not know whether he did this out of extreme severity, or simply to give one of us a chance to defend her. Michael began with the man from Little Russia whom I had questioned the day before. Sophie cast a swift side glance at what was happening on her left, then turned her head away like a woman who tries not to see some indecency committed close by. Four or five times we heard the explosive report, like a wooden box bursting, and it seemed to me that I had never before measured the full horror of that sound. Suddenly Sophie signalled to Michael in the discreet but peremptory manner of a mistress giving a last order to her servant in the presence of guests. Michael obediently walked toward her, half bowing, as stupidly submissive to her request as to the pending order to shoot her; she murmured a few words which I was just too far from her to catch and he answered,

"Yes, Miss Sophie."

The one-time gardener turned back to me again and mumbled in the gruff but deprecating tone of a frightened old servant who knows that he will get himself dismissed for bringing such a message:

"She orders . . . that is, Miss Sophie asks. . . . She wants it to be you. . . ."

He handed me a revolver; I took my own, however, and automatically advanced a step. In that brief space I must have repeated to myself ten times over that Sophie perhaps had a last request to make, and that this order was only a pretext for addressing it to me so that no one could hear. But her lips did not move: hardly aware of what she was doing she had begun to unbutton the upper half of her jacket, as if I were about to press the revolver against her very heart. I must admit that the few thoughts I had at the moment went out to that body, so alive and warm, which the intimacy of our life together had made almost as familiar to me as the body of any soldier friend; and I felt pangs of something like regret, absurdly enough, for the children that this woman might have borne, who would have inherited her courage, and her eyes. Absurd, for who wants to people the stadia and the trenches of the future?

One step more brought me so close to Sophie that I could almost have kissed her bared throat or laid a hand on her shoulder, now visibly shuddering, but by this time she was partly turned from me. She was breathing only slightly too fast; I clung to the thought that I had wanted to put an end to Conrad, and that this was the same thing. I fired, turning my head away like a frightened child setting off a torpedo on Christmas Eve. The first shot did no more than tear open the face, so that I shall never know (and it haunts me still) what expression Sophie would have had in death. On the second shot everything was over.

At first I thought that in asking me to perform this duty she had intended to give me a final proof of her love, the most conclusive proof of all. But I understood afterwards that she only wished to take revenge, leaving me prey to remorse. She was right in that: I do feel remorse at times. One is always trapped, somehow, in dealings with women.